I0570644

Death Stalks
the Forest

David Q. Hall

This is a work of fiction. Names, characters, businesses, places, events and incidents are either the products of the author's imagination or used in a fictitious manner. Any resemblance to actual persons, living or dead, or actual events is purely coincidental.

All rights reserved. This book or any portion thereof may not be reproduced, performed or used in any manner whatsoever without the express written permission of the publisher or author except for the use of brief quotations in a book review.

Printed in the United States of America
First Printing 2020
All rights reserved.

ISBN: 978-1-948894-10-4

Copyright © 2020 by David Q. Hall

Tree Shadow Press

www.treeshadowpress.com

DEDICATION

In memory of "Buck,"
the best tracking teacher I ever knew.

ACKNOWLEDGMENTS

In grateful memory of my father, Bernard "Bill" Hall, who first introduced me to the forest, and his ancestors going back to pre-Revolutionary War times who were recorded as being "renowned hunters and trappers."

CHAPTER ONE

The Angel of Death soared over the surreal scene on the edge of State Highway 72 in Northern Michigan. Down below, the flashing lights of the Michigan State Police patrol car created a strobe-like effect on the otherwise pitch-black highway. At slightly after 2:00 in the morning, traffic was very light, and the first vehicle to approach the scene was still over the next hill, just starting to climb the far slope. A rusty, red pickup truck sped away, spraying gravel and leaving the patrol car sitting on the dark roadside...and the body of state trooper James Baldwin splayed in front of his car, blood spreading onto the asphalt and the gravel edge.

The angel swept down as Officer Baldwin's fading heart fluttered its final, faint beat, and gathered up the soul. It cradled the essence of the dedicated law enforcement officer, faithful husband and loving father of two young girls, and carried him into the eternity of the Kingdom of Heaven. The flashing lights glinted off the handle and the bottom of the long blade left stuck in the chest of the corpse, as the widening pool of blood gave its own bizarre reflections of the red and blue lights.

The driver of the big 18-wheeler that came down the slope and passed by the patrol car glanced over as he drove by and caught a glimpse of trooper Baldwin's dead body in the headlights of the trooper's car. Jolted with a surge of adrenaline, the driver hit the air brakes, grabbed his phone, and called 911.

"911 Operator, please state the nature of your emergency," came the immediate answer.

"Uh, I'm driving a Steelcase delivery truck on State Highway 72, heading east, uh about 5-6 miles out of Kalkaska. I think something's wrong with one of your state troopers."

In truth, nothing would ever be wrong again for James Baldwin. At that very instant he was reunited with his Creator and able to see God face-to-face at last as the Angel of Death brought him before the Eternal Throne of God. The scene left behind on that Northern Michigan roadside was, on the other hand, very, very wrong.

CHAPTER TWO

The rusted-out red Ford 150 truck continued east on Highway 72. When the state highway turned south to head through the village of Kalkaska, the driver continued east on Nash Road. After about five miles, he turned south on Crawford Lake Road and kept going as it turned into North Sharon Road. He was well into the Pere Marquette State Forest lands now and was starting to feel more confident of his get-away. Besides, he always felt more comfortable and capable of meeting any challenge when deep in the forest.

The fatal scuffle with the state police trooper had been regrettable and entirely unnecessary. It was the stupid cop's own fault that he had gotten himself killed.

Okay, the driver thought, *I was driving a bit too fast on the state highway, and, yah, I was high – feeling really good – but all he had to do was write me up and we could have gone our separate ways. But oh, no, he had to be a hard ass about it. Wanted me to get out, walk a line, take a breathalyzer. And shit, if he had looked around in here and come across the meth...Well, I tried to say I'd just take the ticket and bother him no more, but he grabbed me by my shoulder as I turned away, and nobody puts their hands on me. I had to slip my blade out and teach him a lesson. Hell, his eyes sure got big when the cold steel sank into his chest. Woo-ee, I bet he pissed his pants before he hit the ground. I should have pulled my Bowie out and taken it with me, but he just kept clutching the handle with both hands and staring up like he wanted to say something. But all that came out was blood and bubbles. He should have said, "I'm sorry, sir, that I laid my hand on you. I never should have pulled you over in the first place. Go on now and have a nice evening." But no, he had to go and get himself killed, the stupid Smokey. Why does everything have to happen to me? It's goddamned not fair.*

The land on both sides was swampy and the edge of the road was soft sand as he took the turn faster than he should have. The combination of his high, feeling worked up over the stupid cop, and the wet, sandy roadside caused him to skid into the ditch. He was stuck, and no amount of gunning it and spinning his rear tires so much as budged him back toward the road.

Why does everything happen to me? Damn it all. But off in the distance, coming up from the south, he saw headlights.

Crystal Johnson was driving home from closing the *Happy Times Bar* in Lake City. It had been 2:30 in the morning before she had locked up and left, and it was almost thirty miles home to her little lake house on Kniss Lake. The route was always dark and deserted looking, but she had done it for years now, and at least she could sleep late that morning. She didn't have to be back to work at the bar-restaurant until 6:00 the next evening.

As Crystal drove down the hill toward the low, swampy area near the North Branch of the Manistee River, her headlights caught the form of the pickup truck angled into the wet ditch, obviously stuck. The driver was out, standing near the edge of the road, waving in her direction.

She slowed and thought. *I'm alone. This is not the time to stop for a stranger on a deserted, dark, gravel road back in the woods. I should just phone in a road emergency call to 911.* But as she drew closer, the fellow looked kind of familiar as he spread his arms out in a pleading gesture. It was part of the ingrained culture of the North Woods of Michigan that you didn't leave someone stranded.

You stopped to help.

You had to be a good neighbor.

Crystal slowed to a stop and the man walked over to her open driver's side window.

"Golle-e-e," he exclaimed, "I didn't think anybody would be along this way until morning. I'm sure glad you stopped."

His appreciative manner instantly started to put Crystal more at ease. She knew she was doing the right thing, stopping to help the poor guy.

"Do you want me to give you a ride? I'm heading farther north. It might not be until later tomorrow morning before any roadside assistance would get out here."

"That'd sure be neighborly of you," the fellow seemed so friendly. "And I'm sorry to put you to more trouble, but do you suppose you could help me carry some of my stuff from my truck? I don't want to leave it here where somebody might come along and help themselves. You know what I mean, the way some of these backwoods folks help themselves to whatever they come across."

A little warning flag popped up in the back of Crystal's mind that she shouldn't leave her position behind the steering wheel of her old, scratched Oldsmobile. She could still gun it and drive off if he seemed at all threatening. But she pushed it back down. What he said was right. Some survivalists, hermits and recluses in this vast forest would be inclined to help themselves to anything of value on a deserted roadside. She opened her driver's door and started to get out.

"Sure," she said agreeably. "I'll give a hand."

It was the last thing she would be able to say for many hours, as the man grabbed her from behind, held a gloved hand over her mouth so firmly that she couldn't so much as make a noise, and wrestled her easily over to his truck. Keeping his hand over her mouth, he let go of her with his other hand, but before she could try to break free of his grip, everything went black.

CHAPTER THREE

Michigan State Police Trooper Andrea Henriks and her husband of two years, the Rev. Dr. Danny Henriks, sat down at the kitchen table of their home in East Bay Township just outside of Traverse City, Michigan.

"Wow, do you look sharp this morning," Danny exclaimed as Andrea pulled up her chair. "Sharply pressed uniform, ribbons and everything. Have some function to attend?"

"I'm afraid so," Andrea responded with a frown. "You remember my fellow trooper, Officer Baldwin, who was murdered last Friday night on the side of the road outside Kalkaska?"

"Oh, yeah, that was horrible. Left a widow and two little girls, as I recall."

"Yes, just tragic. Well, his funeral is today, so we're all turning out to honor his life and years of service. The funeral will be at my old church where I grew up, Central United Methodist in Traverse City, with interment at Grand

Traverse Memorial Gardens on Veterans Drive."

"That's just so sad," Danny shook his head. "From what I've heard on the news, I guess you guys still haven't figured out who did it, how it happened?"

"The investigation is, as we say, ongoing, but no, no arrest has been made. Plaster casts were made of the other vehicle's tire tracks, but the tread was pretty worn down. The pattern indicates Bridgestone make, with one odd tire that may be a retread...so could be an older vehicle, maybe a light truck or SUV of some kind, but maybe not with its original tires."

"What about tracks from the perpetrator?"

"From what I hear," Andrea replied, "there was only a partial print in the gravel berm. The perp probably stayed mostly on the pavement when he exited his vehicle. The partial was a rather deep tread, probably a hunting- or hiking-type boot, with a ragged notch on the outside edge of the left sole. Forensics at the Grayling lab are trying to run down a possible manufacturer, but if it turns out to be a common make, like Redwing, Rocky or Wolverine...well, all kinds of retailers up here sell those, so identifying the boot might not provide much of a lead."

"No witnesses, I suppose," Danny said glumly.

"No, certainly not of the murder itself, nor of any vehicle leaving the scene. It was called in by the driver of an 18-wheeler, but the fellow – who was really shook up – reported to officers responding that he didn't see anything but the patrol car, lights still flashing, and Trooper Baldwin's dead body. No sign of the vehicle he must have pulled over in the wee hours of Saturday morning. The forensics team and the medical examiner have been examining Baldwin's hands, his uniform, everything they can, to try to find even the smallest amount of trace evidence."

"They think that he must have come into direct contact

with his murderer, then."

"Well, yeah," Andrea chided Danny, "after all, he was stabbed with a long-bladed hunting knife. So obviously Baldwin and his killer must have grappled, however briefly."

"Well, I'm truly sorry," Danny replied. "My prayers today will be sure to include Officer Baldwin, his family, your entire State Police family, and, of course, you, my love...as I pray for you every day."

"And I for you," Andrea smiled with her brilliantly beautiful smile that always made his heart flutter. "And what's on your schedule for today?"

"Today I have to drive up to the Mackinac Presbytery office, do some paperwork at my desk there, meet in the afternoon with the presbytery Mission Committee's subcommittee for awarding grants to worthy projects, catch some supper at the Grand Traverse Pie Company in Petoskey with the presbytery stated clerk, Joe, and stop by the First Presbyterian Church in Elk Rapids for part of their third Monday of the month Session meeting this evening before driving home."

"So, it'll be a typically late night for you," Andrea concluded.

"Well, I don't have to stay for the whole meeting with their elders. They'll have me first on the docket, right after call to order, invocation, reading of Scripture, and whatever else they do for opening devotions, so I'm hopeful of being out of there by 7:30. Maybe I'll even be home by 8:00?" Danny shrugged optimistically.

"While I won't hold my breath on that," Andrea said, knowing full well how unpredictable, long-winded, and boring church meetings could be. "Whatever time you get home, I'll be waiting. And what I have in mind will take *your* breath away." She gave him her best *come hither* look and winked seductively.

"You are so-o sexy when you do that, and in uniform, too," he laughed. And they embraced and held each other hard for a long, passionate kiss. Neither could imagine any love that could be stronger or better than what they had for each other. The Angel of Providence and Protection had brought them together over two years ago; they had quickly fallen deeply in love, and less than two months later they had married in a joint wedding service with two of their best friends in the entire world, Will "Tiny" Jones and his sensationally gorgeous wife, Angela.

Danny watched lovingly as Andrea walked out the door, her blonde hair pulled back tightly and tucked up in her broad-brimmed trooper's hat, but curling wisps sticking out behind. He could not imagine a more beautiful and loving woman anywhere in the world. He admired the strength and confidence she exhibited – both in her work as a complete professional, and in their life together as wife and husband. It seemed unbelievable to Danny that one woman could so completely combine the qualities of competence and compassion, strength and softness, grace and, well...guts.

When the two of them had been under fire that terrible night on the Mackinac Bridge – when Ken Romano had tried yet again to murder him in behalf of Ken's sick, twisted sister, Sarah – Andrea hadn't hesitated a moment to confront the shooter and duel it out with him. And out of all the men in the world, she had fallen in love with Daniel Henriks and married him to be her life-partner.

Miraculous, he thought. And it was.

CHAPTER FOUR

As Danny drove the same Highway 72 east toward Kalkaska, before turning north there up U.S. Highway 131 to Petoskey, he passed the spot where Trooper Baldwin had been murdered. Someone – likely family members, relatives, friends, or even just caring people who had heard of the tragedy – had planted crosses, plastic flowers, and small objects including a teddy bear, to memorialize him at the roadside. A naturally inquisitive and frankly rather compulsive man by nature, Danny indulged in the thought that he should pull over and look over the scene himself. If he had done so and actually spotted a missed clue, it would not have been the first time he had done so at a murder scene.

Approximately five years before, when Danny had been pastor of the South Presbyterian Church in Pittsburgh, Pennsylvania, his best friend at that time, Bill Brand, had been murdered by his scorned wife, Sarah Brand. She had planned meticulously and staged the murder carefully to make it look as though the Rev. Dr. Bill Brand had committed suicide in the Rector's Study of his own church, Church of the Resurrection, in the upper-crust neighborhood of Shadyside in Pittsburgh. All evidence had seemed to the most skilled police investigators to point to Bill taking his life by sticking the muzzle of his own shotgun in his mouth and pressing the trigger with his big toe. But when Danny came into the crime scene shortly after it had happened, he had noticed a small detail of the shotgun that Sarah had failed to get just right. And eventually it had come out that she was the perpetrator of Bill's death.

But he resisted the temptation to stop by the spot of Trooper Baldwin's death. He had a busy work day ahead of him, and he wanted to get to the presbytery office in the Mitchell Park area of Petoskey by no later than 8:30. The thought did cross his mind as he drove by, however, that whoever the murderer was, he had to be either very skilled or very lucky to get the drop on a veteran state trooper like Baldwin. It would not have been easy to get close enough to plunge a hunting knife into Baldwin's chest. And it seemed to Danny that if someone felt the need to kill the officer, a gun would have been a more obvious choice of weapon. It had to be someone who had confidence in wielding a big knife...perhaps a military veteran well-trained in hand-to-hand combat, or a knife collector/connoisseur...or better, a dedicated survivalist or expert hunter, both of whom were quite common in the extensive forests of Northern Michigan.

He had received a number of hard lessons over the years that he should leave crime investigation up to the professionals, but frankly, Danny couldn't help himself. It's not that he had ambitions of being an amateur private detective. He just had a drive to find out and learn the answers to all kinds of questions, including mysteries. Even those involving murder.

But he drove on, turning his mind toward the work on his schedule for the day. It was mid-October. In a month, he would reach his second anniversary as the Interim Executive Presbyter of the Presbytery of Mackinac, including 42 congregations in the Upper Peninsula and northern Lower Peninsula of Michigan. Although his position was officially temporary, the search process for a permanent Executive Presbyter had proceeded slowly. Truth be known, most of the pastors and elder representatives in the Presbytery were very pleased with the job Danny was doing, and they really weren't in a hurry to replace him.

The duties of executive presbyters in the regional presbyteries of the Presbyterian Church in the United States of America were largely administrative, with lots of meetings and office work, but what Danny found most fulfilling was being what was often referred to as a "pastor to pastors" and a "shepherd" to the congregations of Mackinac Presbytery. Now approaching 60, he had many years of experience in Presbyterian churches.

Almost unanimously, the pastors and churches of Mackinac recognized that Danny had no personal or professional agenda other than trying to be helpful and supportive to them, so more than once there had been a groundswell to make him the permanent EP, but he had always declined the possibility. He frankly didn't know just how much longer he really wanted to work such long and demanding hours. Retirement and more part-time ministry were looking more and more appealing to him. Besides, there was nothing he wanted more than to be available to his beloved wife, Andrea. She was usually home from her work as a state trooper in the evenings, and he hated the fact that so many of his evenings were involved in church meetings and apart from her.

CHAPTER FIVE

As usual, Andrea had been right. The discussion at the meeting of the elders of First Presbyterian Church of Elk Rapids had dragged on later than Danny had hoped, and even though the outcome was positive and they had liked what he had to share with them, it was 9:00 P.M. by the time he got home. Nevertheless, as she had promised, Andrea was waiting for him with warm embrace, passionate kiss...and both a bottle of her favorite Michigan Riesling and a bottle of his Crown Royal Black Canadian whiskey. And she looked sensational in her comfortable sweats, moccasins, and her blonde curls down to her shoulders. Now in her late 40's, while little wisps of gray were occurring naturally in her wavy hair, she preferred to maintain her blonde color. He thought she looked superbly beautiful however she decided to wear her hair, and she always had a sparkling smile that could stop traffic.

As she sipped her wine and he his whiskey, neat, Andrea asked, "Did you listen to the news on your car radio driving home this evening?"

"No," Danny replied. "Frankly, after a long day and over an hour of discussion with the Elk Rapids folks, I just wanted to listen to classical music on the Interlochen public radio station. Why do you ask?"

"Well, as you know, I went to James Baldwin's funeral service this morning – there was a terrific turnout, by the way, and it was a very fitting tribute for him – but while we were there at Central Methodist, word started to spread among the troopers that there was a fast-breaking development that may be related to his murder."

"Really?" Danny sat forward in his chair. "What was it?"

"A Kalkaska deputy sheriff was patrolling late Sunday down on Sharon Road where it's all forest, and he came upon a rusty, old, red Ford pickup that had been driving south at what must have been high speed, obviously skidded on wet gravel, and went into the roadside ditch in a low area near the North Branch of the Manistee River."

"And it was connected to Trooper Baldwin's murder?" Danny asked.

"The deputy noticed that three of the tires on the pickup were worn Bridgestones, not much tread, with an odd tire on the right rear. It rang a bell with him since he had gotten our state police bulletin on the investigation of Baldwin's murder, so he called in to dispatch and a crime scene investigation team got out there. They made comparisons to photos of the tread found leaving the scene of the murder, and it was a match. But that's not all."

Danny perked up even more, "What else?"

Andrea went on, "There were tracks in the wet sand and gravel made by deep-lugged hunting boots, and the left sole had a ragged notch torn in the Vibram. That also was a match to the partial boot track left on the berm of Highway 72 where Baldwin was stabbed."

"So," Danny deduced, "it sounds likely that the driver of the red pickup fled the scene of the murder of Trooper Baldwin, made his way south and east to Sharon Road, was driving too fast on the wet sand and gravel, and skidded into that ditch where he was stuck and couldn't get his vehicle out."

"Yup," Andrea affirmed, "and he gave us leads to follow up on that we wouldn't have had otherwise. And there's yet another interesting detail."

"Oh, there's even more?"

Andrea leaned forward, "The pickup belongs to our old 'friend,' Wes Smith."

Danny felt stunned. "No kidding...Wes Smith, huh?"

Both Andrea and Danny remembered well that a little over two years before, Wes Smith had been an allegedly unwitting accomplice in Ken Romano's attempt to shoot Danny out on the sporting clays course of the Cedar Rod & Gun Club west and north of Traverse City. As Ken had made his unsuccessful shot with his .308 scoped rifle, Wes had simultaneously created a diversion by running past the range house, jumping into his rusty, red pickup truck, and speeding off...thus drawing attention to himself while Ken had slipped away unnoticed.

Sheriff deputies' subsequent investigation and interviews of Wes had concluded that he was ignorant of Ken's intent and plan, gullibly accepting that Ken's shot was supposed to be a prank to scare a friend out on the range, and the only thing he had been found guilty of was a misdemeanor for creating a public disturbance. Danny also remembered that Andrea had said back then that she had pulled Wes over a couple of times for speeding and DUI, that he and his game violator brothers were scofflaws, but none of them had ever been arrested for any violent acts.

Danny mulled over what Andrea had just told him and

what he remembered from the Cedar Club shooting incident and went on.

"Do you suppose the Leelanau County Sheriff's investigators were wrong about Wes? Could he have been in cahoots with Ken Romano all along in trying to kill me? Maybe he has a more violent streak in him than anyone suspected. Although it seems strange that he would murder Trooper Baldwin as a result of an early morning traffic stop. You said he was never hostile or belligerent when you pulled him over for speeding. There has to be more to it than the threat of a speeding ticket."

"I agree," Andrea replied, "and from what I've heard, the forensics team in Grayling is just now going over the pickup with the proverbial fine-tooth comb. I'll let you know what, if anything, they find that would connect Wes with Baldwin's death. And if it was Wes who was driving his truck when it got stuck there by the North Branch, he had a companion, probably a woman."

"How do you know that?" Danny asked.

"There were tracks of a smaller size in the sand near the stuck truck. But neither the guy's tracks nor the woman's were found going anywhere away from the truck. They had to have been picked up by someone who came along on Sharon Road...or else they took off into the thick forest and left the truck there. But that's not likely."

"Why not?"

"Since it was quickly determined that the pickup had been at the scene of Trooper Baldwin's murder and was undoubtedly driven by his murderer," Andrea explained, "a whole team of investigators and tracking dogs were brought to the place where the truck had gotten stuck. Now it was the better part of two days after the murder that the truck was found by the deputy, but conditions had been dry, so there was at least a chance that the dogs could pick up scent of the two leaving the scene. Plus, of course, veteran trackers scoured the vicinity of the pickup looking for a trail leading away, but there was nothing."

"So," Danny summed it up, "they must have left the pickup by means of some vehicle that came along."

"Yup," she agreed, "or…"

"Or what?"

"Well, from what I've heard, near the pickup the woman's tracks were scuffled. It was impossible to tell if she was just dashing around the front of the truck, or if possibly she had been grabbed by the man and there had been a brief struggle."

Danny pondered that possibility. "So, one potential theory could be that she drove the vehicle that enabled the murderer to get away from his stuck truck. That she came along, stopped to try to help, and got snatched by a man desperate to make an escape. But back in Pittsburgh where I used to live and work, I can't imagine a lone woman – or pretty much anyone, for that matter – stopping for a man on a roadside late on a dark night. What woman would do that?"

"Someone up here in Northern Michigan who is a good neighbor," Andrea replied. "You don't leave even strangers stranded deep in the forest. You have to try to help."

"Well, if that happens to be the scenario of what happened there on North Sharon Road that night, where are they? And what's happened to the poor woman?"

"We have no way of knowing. I actually hope that she was an accomplice, and that eventually we'll find both of them. I hate to think," Andrea scowled, "that there could be a second murder involved in this tragedy."

CHAPTER SIX

The next day, the Tuesday after Officer James Baldwin's murder, Danny had no meetings scheduled and had decided to work at home instead of driving to the Presbytery Office in Petoskey. Andrea had patrol duties close to Traverse City, but a light schedule herself, so they decided to meet for lunch at the Grand Traverse Pie Company on West Front Street.

"Say, how 'bout I give Tiny a call and see if he's available to meet us for a chicken pot pie or something?" Danny suggested. "Or in his case, two or three," he laughed. Tiny was six foot five and weighed well over 300 pounds, a former defensive lineman for the University of Pittsburgh Panthers, and even though he was in his early 60's, his appetite was still formidable.

"Sounds great," Andrea smiled. "I wish Angela could join us, but it's too far for her to leave the shop in Suttons Bay and get back again in just an hour."

"Well, if Tiny can lunch with us, we could talk with him

about the four of us doing something this week. Angela's shop closes on Wednesdays now that we're in the last half of October and the fall color tourists are winding down. They tend to be busier on the weekends."

"Okay, that'd be wonderful. Let me know if there's any change, otherwise I'll see you at noon." She flashed that sparkling smile, gave him a strong hug and kiss, and was out the door.

Danny straightened up the kitchen and put their dishes in the dishwasher while his mind turned to Tiny. The two had been best friends while they still lived and worked in Pittsburgh, Pennsylvania. They had been on vacation together in late August, just over two years ago, when Tiny had met Angela for the first time while he browsed in her gift shop in Suttons Bay, north and west of Traverse City on the beautiful Leelanau Peninsula. The same day Danny had met Andrea when they each went to the Cedar Rod & Gun Club to target shoot on the sporting clays course. Remarkably, that week the two men had fallen in love with the two women, respectively, proposed marriage, and were married in a joint wedding in the Presbyterian Church of Traverse City the first Saturday of the following October. The four had been best of friends ever since, even spending the first few days of their honeymoons together on Mackinac Island.

By the first of that November, Tiny had completed the sale of his business ventures in the Hill District of Pittsburgh to his long-time associates, Slick and Speed. He moved permanently to Suttons Bay, where he lived with Angela, in her spacious and attractive apartment. Angela continued to keep the books and work the counter of Sam and Julie's gift shop. Tiny, meanwhile, had started up "Tiny's Big Security Services" in an office in Traverse City, where he did some of the same things he had done back in Pittsburgh – selling, maintaining, and monitoring security systems for various businesses and private residences, providing security patrols and checks for absentee owners, and putting on security seminars and informational programs for a wide variety of groups in the area.

While it's not unusual for start-up businesses to take a few years to begin operating "in the black," if they survive in the first place, Tiny had gotten a good foothold in the Grand Traverse area within the first year. With Angela's help and bookkeeping starting out, he had made enough sales and earned enough fees not only to break even within a year's time, but also to add a couple of employees...which helped immensely with both operating his office and conducting security checks and patrols for paying clients. After almost two years, he even had two company cars – Jeep Wranglers decked out with special lights, electronics, and painted in Pitt Panther colors of gold and blue with the lettering on the doors, *Tiny's Big Security Services*.

The coloring was close enough that most people assumed it was maize and blue for the University of Michigan, which made a positive connection with so many U of M alums and fans in the area. It also gave him the idea of adding one or two more Jeeps painted in Spartan green and white, a psychological appeal for the also numerous alums and fans of the Michigan State University. Tiny had an almost instinctive knack for marketing, and made an invariably positive impression in any setting, whether one-on-one with prospective clients or before large audiences. It didn't hurt that he could play the proverbial "genial giant" with little children and their parents. "Big Tiny Will Keep You and Yours Safe"...or the massive, menacing monster, "Burglars Beware – Big Tiny is On the Job."

In just those two years he had become something of an instant celebrity in the several counties of the Northwestern Lower Peninsula, which was no surprise to Angela, having seen what a genuine folk hero her husband had been in the Hill District and its slum-ghetto neighborhoods. He even landed a weekly spot on channels 7&4 television, a 10-minute morning item they entitled, "Big Tiny's Tips for Security" in the home and business. Such quick success had not changed him in the least, however. What mattered most to Will "Tiny" Jones was his love for the incredibly beautiful Angela and his loyalty to his few closest friends, especially Andrea and Danny. Truth be told, he looked up to and admired Danny for the quality of man he was. There was no deception, no falseness, and no checkered integrity with the Rev. Dr. Daniel Henriks, which was almost unknown in the environment in which Tiny had been born, lived and worked all his years on the Hill. He would do anything for Danny.

Danny called Tiny's number. The phone rang twice, and the big guy answered. He had an administrative assistant by now, but unless he was with a client, he preferred that people got to talk to him as soon as they called.

"Hey, Danny, Tiny's Big Security Services here. What's happening?"

"Good morning, Big Tiny," Danny answered, playing along with his best friend. "You available for lunch today at noon with me and the world's most beautiful woman?"

"Angela's going to be in TC for lunch? You bet!"

"You know I meant Andrea, funny man, but I wish Angela was here to join us."

"Yah," Tiny agreed. "But she doesn't have enough of a lunch break to get down here. But sure, I can meet you two. Where you wanta go?"

"Pie Company on the west side...for pot pies and your favorite Northern Spy apple pie. And I'm buying," Danny offered.

"Katrina," Tiny called to his assistant, "I'm going to lunch now. The Rev. Dr. Henriks is buying today, and I want to be there before he gets there, so's I don't miss out."

Danny could hear Katrina's response in the background. "You go right ahead, Tiny. I can handle everything that comes in, as usual. But you better get take-out for me, if Dr. Henriks is buying."

Tiny pretended to take down her order. "And that'll be an entire broccoli-cheddar quiche and an apple pie for Katrina. How 'bout something to take home for supper, Kat?"

"Okay," Danny laughed, "something for Katrina, too. You know, Big Tiny, you're supposed to be providing protection services, not rip-offs of your long-suffering friends."

Tiny roared in his usual exuberant style. "You got that reversed, homey, *I'm* the long-suffering one. How many times have I had to rescue your sorry ass? I'm just collecting on a long-standing debt that will never be paid off," he kidded.

Danny knew that he was just busting his chops, but he turned serious for a moment. "You're absolutely right, big guy. I can never repay what you've done for me over the years."

"And you'll never have to," Tiny himself turned serious. "Anything I've done for you has been paid for in advance by your friendship. You can cash in that chip an infinite number of times going forward. I'm always here for you, Danny. Noon it is."

Danny reflected on Tiny's love and loyalty for him. It was his essential nature to reflect on and ponder over all matters of life and the cosmos. It was surely out of nothing less than the pure grace of God that he experienced all levels of love in his life at this point. Like most people, he had things, possessions that he loved in a sense – his home, his young English Springer Spaniel bird dog, his favorite chair, his shotguns and fly rods for trout fishing, and a number of other prized possessions. With the divine gift of Andrea, he realized the combination of both the most beautiful sexual love imaginable, what the ancient Greeks called "*eros*," and the deepest, highest friendship possible among human beings, in Greek, "*philia*." And in Tiny he had another expression of *philia*, "brotherly love." Finally, he was always conscious of the absolute love of God for himself. That divine Love was pure gift. He could never be or do enough to deserve it or earn it. It was his out of the grace of the Creator God who is Love. There was nothing that he could do but be thankful and never take any of his loves for granted. And that included his best friend who was not his spouse, Tiny.

CHAPTER SEVEN

Approximately three-and-a-half hours later, Andrea, Tiny and Danny met at the Grand Traverse Pie Company. Andrea gave a little hug and kiss to Danny, turned to Tiny, and was immediately enveloped by a huge bear hug. Nearby patrons turned and undoubtedly wondered who this big fellow was who presumed to give such a vigorous hug to a State Police Trooper in her uniform. But they smiled as well.

The three placed their orders, including a take-out slice of quiche and a slice of apple pie for Katrina, and Danny paid as he promised. They chose a table in the back room where they could talk more quietly. After the initial "Well, how's it going?" and "How ya been?" Andrea raised the question of whether Tiny and Angela could be available to do something with Danny and her Wednesday afternoon, after his Bible Study group at church and brunch out somewhere.

"I know Angie and I don't have anything on our schedule," Tiny said. "We can call her before we split from each other after our lunch, but I'm pretty sure you can count us in. Did you have something in mind?"

Danny jumped in, "It's a drizzly Tuesday now, but the week's weather forecast is for tomorrow to be really pleasant: sunny, mid-60's..."

"Yeah," Andrea interrupted, "so we should do something outside. We're almost to the last week of October. The fall color is still beautiful, even though leaves are dropping every day."

"I was thinking," Danny took back his line of thought, "Andrea's late uncle Jake had an old, 19th century, log cabin way back in the woods down in Kalkaska County. I remember, hon, that you said it was left to you and you had keys for it, but you hadn't actually been there to see it for a number of years. But I know we pay taxes on it twice a year."

"That's right," Andrea agreed. "I've thought for some time that we should go there, check it out, see if we would ever want to use it...or just put it up for sale...whatever. But ever since we've been married, we've been so busy buying our own house, moving in, trying to sort through all the stuff I had in my old condo, all your stuff from your home in Pittsburgh. And getting used to your new job with Mackinac Presbytery, and now my new duties with the TNT..."

"TNT?" Tiny wondered.

"The Traverse Narcotics Team unit," Andrea explained. "After I declined the promotion offered me downstate just before Danny proposed, and I decided to stay up here in Traverse City to make our life together here, our Post Commander, Lieutenant Wade..."

"I remember him from being in our wedding," Tiny interrupted. "Sorry, go on."

"He came to me and asked me to start training for the Narcotics Team, that he wanted one of his best and most experienced officers to take that open position. I still do patrol duty, but I rotate off whenever investigation and action are needed with narcotics operations. Which reminds me..."

"Of what?" Danny asked.

"Well," she continued, "remember I said I'd keep you posted on the Trooper Baldwin investigation – including what, if anything, the Grayling forensics lab found in going over Wes Smith's old pickup truck. The only prints they found were those of Wes, although they think the driver of it who killed Baldwin was wearing gloves at the time. Anyway, they also found trace amounts of methamphetamines in the cab of the truck."

Tiny flashed instant recognition. "Meth was a big problem on the Hill back in Pittsburgh. My boys and I kept the lid on pretty tight in our 'hood' when it came to crack cocaine and heroin, but gang boys were frequently trying to set up meth labs in abandoned buildings, garages, wherever they could."

"Well," Andrea went on, "as you know, meth is in the class of phenethylamine drugs and produces potent psycho-stimulation..."

"Hold on, dear," Danny broke in, "I'm afraid your training in the TNT is overwhelming this naïve boy."

Andrea smiled a bit awkwardly, "Sorry. Anyway, bottom line is that the lab team thinks that not only was the driver a user of meth, but given its traces around the truck cab, he was probably producing it, and using the pickup to transport it in some quantity. Maybe part of a distribution network going downstate to more urban areas like Grand Rapids, Lansing, Ann Arbor, Detroit, and elsewhere."

"So poor Baldwin's death is both a murder investigation and a drug task force investigation," Danny concluded. "Will that mean that you'll have to work on this tomorrow?"

"No, we're conferencing Thursday and Friday to broaden the investigation even farther – although it's hard to imagine it becoming even more intense when the murder of a fellow trooper is involved – and it probably won't be until Friday that we know plans and parameters that will impact my duties and schedule. Oh, but there's been another breaking development in the case,"

"What now?" Danny wondered, as Tiny leaned forward with great interest himself.

"Yesterday, late Monday afternoon, yet another deputy patrolling back roads in Kalkaska County, deep into the forest, spotted recent tracks down a two-rutted lane and decided to follow them. He figured that it was probably upland bird hunters or bow hunters looking for deer, but everything is being checked ever more closely, trying to get leads on Baldwin's killer. Off of South Sharon Road, to the east near Big Cannon Creek, he came across a recently burned-out, previously white Oldsmobile sedan."

"He called for a crime scene investigation team and dogs with their handlers when he spotted a few tracks in a nearby puddle of water – that hunting boot with the tear in the sole, and those belonging to a smaller foot size, likely a woman. They were headed into the thick alders along the creek and seemed to disappear into the water and muck. The dogs lost the scent, of course, but they searched for more tracks and scent both upstream and down. They're out there today. Still searching. And we have our State Police helicopter doing overhead search."

"Any speculation as to whether the woman is an accomplice or a captive?" Danny wondered.

"As before, impossible to say. But the car was abandoned and torched before dawn last week Saturday, a few hours after Baldwin's murder. If the woman was kidnapped and her car hijacked for the killer to try to get away from the stuck pickup truck...well, he may have decided that she is too much of a burden there in the thick forest and that he needs neither a hostage nor a witness. Besides, he undoubtedly has a quantity of meth that he has to tote in his getaway. I wish I could be more optimistic about the lady."

"I have to admit," Danny said, "that I don't know the area nearly as well as you do, dear, but wouldn't that search be taking place in the general vicinity of your late uncle's cabin?"

"Some miles away," Andrea replied. "The cabin is off to the west, actually in what's known as South Swamp. Prevailing theory about the perpetrator and the woman is that they disappeared in the Big Devil Swamp...or made their way down Big Cannon Creek to the Big Manistee River. There are lots of cottages and cabins along the Big Manistee where they could steal a canoe to make a getaway by river, eventually pulling out miles away at a major road. Or, if they found a place that had already been closed up for the winter, they could break in and lie low for a while. Lots of people have canned goods and dry food stored in their cottages, so they could potentially wait for days or weeks for the search to die down."

"So, you don't think there's a problem with going to your uncle's cabin for the afternoon tomorrow?" Tiny asked.

"No, the dragnet doesn't extend that far to the west. Dog handlers and search teams are concentrating on about a three-mile radius of where the old Oldsmobile was found near Big Cannon. If they can't find them over there, or at least pick up a trail to follow, well, who knows where they might be in this vast Northern Michigan forest?"

"Then let's plan on the four of us checking out your Uncle Jake's old cabin tomorrow after my Bible study," Danny said enthusiastically.

"Sounds good to me," Tiny agreed.

Andrea added, "And to save time, instead of going out for brunch, why don't we pack a picnic lunch? Maybe roast some hot dogs at Uncle's cabin."

"I'll call Angela to make sure," Tiny said, "but count us in."

"Super," Danny responded. "The weather forecast is for a beautiful late-October day. We'll have a fun and relaxing day of it."

"Oh," Andrea remembered, "tell Angie to wear hiking clothes and boots. At Uncle's cabin we always had to park among the tall trees on high ground, and then follow maybe a quarter-mile trail through thick brush down to the creek bottom. The cabin is tucked deep into a cedar swamp, its back end up against a bank going up from the flood plain of the creek to higher ground. You practically have to run into it with your nose even to know it's there, it's so well hidden. But the setting is lovely. The cedar swamp creek runs by it a few yards beyond the front door and it's full of gorgeous little brook trout. It's the most peaceful and quiet place in all seasons, but you can't beat the beauty now with fall color."

Tiny smiled broadly. "It sounds great, and with the hike involved and the cookout, it'll be a mini-adventure, as well as a much-needed break from all the tension of the past week."

CHAPTER EIGHT

*T*his *woman is slowing me down,* thought the murderer. *At least the duct tape over her mouth keeps her from screaming and all I have to put up with are her stupid whimpers. Well, I couldn't leave her where the cops could find her and ask her questions about me. Maybe it would have been better to have killed her and hidden her body in the stream where their damned dogs couldn't scent her. But I may still have a use for her...and, damn, that's a nice rack on her. She's not a bad looker. If I do have to waste her, at least we can have some fun first.*

It was now between four and five hours since he had left his favorite blade sticking in the chest of the stupid state trooper. *Damn, I loved that knife. What a waste having to leave it in that cop. Well, I have others that'll do what needs doing, whether gutting out a deer...or a pig.*

He laughed to himself at his joke. Sunrise would be in about half an hour, and he wanted them to be invisible to any searchers by then.

The police dragnet would undoubtedly concentrate on the county roads around the tiny town of Sharon – Fletcher, Military, and South, West and North Sharon. As soon as they figured out that he had taken to the water of Big Cannon Creek to throw off any tracking dogs, they would assume that he and the stupid woman had struggled downstream to the Big Manistee, where they could more easily escape from the area.

But, I'm too smart for them, he thought smugly. *They might never figure out what happened to me. Or what I did to her.*

Instead, he literally dragged Crystal upstream, wrestling her over log jams and through soft, mucky creek bottom, but sticking to the water and leaving no scent. He had the advantage of having hip boots available in the pickup, so he was fine for the bit more than a mile they plowed through the water in the dark. Knowing the forest like the proverbial back of his hand, he finally left the creek, dragged her through thick, wet, jungle-like alders, and they crossed under Maples Road by means of a large culvert. Sticking to low, wet, ground, he quickly wrestled her into the depths of Little Cannon Creek Swamp. The authorities would never think that he would go in that direction.

***

By now Crystal Johnson was thoroughly wet, muddy, and coated with fine, black muck from her waist down. She was shivering non-stop from hypothermia, and the duct tape over her mouth made breathing difficult. She had given up on struggling or any attempt to flee because her earlier efforts after she came to resulted in hard blows to her cheeks from her captor. She just wanted this nightmare to be over, this night to be over. She wanted to be warm again. She had no idea where they were, just that they were deep in the forest and sticking to streams and wet, swampy places. He seemed to know where they were headed, and navigated by a small, low-intensity flashlight that couldn't be detected from more than a few yards away and a clip-on compass that he consulted occasionally. *He obviously cares more for his stuffed backpack than he does for me,* she thought.

God, what does he want from me? Crystal wailed silently to herself. *He didn't even bother looking in my purse, so it's not money. The total mess I am, it couldn't be sex. No man would find me attractive this way. He torched my car, so he didn't want that. He keeps bitching and moaning about what a drag I am, how I'm slowing him down. So why is he bothering with me? But every time I fall and am too exhausted even to get up, he doesn't leave me lost in the forest, but wrestles me back to my feet and pushes me on. I just want to lie down. Maybe I'll just die here, then he'd leave me.*

He reached Little Cannon Creek, forced her back into the flowing water, and they splashed downstream a few hundred yards. The icy water was so cold that Crystal's feet and lower legs were completely numb, and the hypothermia made her teeth chatter behind the duct tape. Without compassion he pushed her on, acting frustrated that she was losing control over her legs and balance. But finally, they left the creek itself and entered South Swamp. The eastern sky was getting lighter, but they were almost there and should be hidden away before the sun was up.

***

He could have been there long ago, warming by the wood stove and congratulating himself on his escape if it hadn't been for the uncooperative woman. *She just doesn't want to do what I say,* he thought resentfully. *She's deliberately trying to delay me so they can capture me. Damn them all. It isn't fair that everyone is against me. What did I ever do to that trooper that he had to pick on me? What have I done to deserve the burden of this hateful woman? Maybe I should have killed her and left her in the swamp. When we get there, I'll stick her in the cache until I decide what to do with her. Maybe give her a wash pan so she can clean herself off so's we can have some fun. Damn she's clumsy, but it's just up ahead, so I'll soon be done with her contrariness. Women are such a drag...unless they're on their backs,* he chuckled to himself.

***

Crystal was on the verge of unconsciousness and her shivers were becoming convulsions, but she saw the cabin a few yards ahead through half-closed eyes and somehow felt a flicker of hope. At least maybe he would take her inside. Maybe she could feel warmth again eventually. Maybe the night would finally be over. Maybe she would live another day...maybe.

CHAPTER NINE

He opened the door of the cabin by knocking hard on the padlock with an iron bar, popping the lock open, and literally threw Crystal in on the floor. She moaned and convulsed in the throes of severe hypothermia as he ignored her and set about lighting a small fire in the woodstove in the main room of the cabin. His woodcraft was superb, and he knew expertly how to make a small, clean-burning fire that put out very little smoke to signal that anyone was in the cabin. Nonetheless, as the fire took hold, he stepped back out and gazed upward at the top of the small chimney. Just a wisp of light-colored smoke wafted upward and was quickly dispersed by the light breeze there in the swamp.

Perfect, he thought. *No one could detect that smoke unless they were standing right next to the cabin.*

He went back inside and found Crystal passed out from her ordeal, her muscles twitching involuntarily. *Good,* he thought. *At least she's not bitching and moaning this way.* He left her there in the center of the floor for the time being.

The glow of the rising sun was gradually making the eastern sky brighter, but it wasn't quite sunup yet. Besides, even when the sun was higher in mid-morning, the interior of the cabin remained semi-dark. The cedar and fir trees of the swamp shaded the cabin heavily, and there was very little open sky visible above the little structure. There was no electricity, which was fine with him, since use of electrical power would be a tip-off that someone was in the place. He could have lighted a small, fuel-powered lantern to light up the inside, but passed on it in favor of a single candle for now. He kept the sole window in the main room heavily shaded so that the candlelight couldn't be seen outside. When he left the cabin even for a short time, he usually locked the crude, heavy shutter over the window from both inside and out. That way, it couldn't be opened by someone trying to enter the cabin...nor by someone trying to get out of the place.

There was a good stock of canned and dry foods in the rough cupboards of the cabin, and he decided that he had worked up a real appetite, slogging his way through miles of flowing creek, soft, wet sand and muck, and thick swamp brush...all the time dragging along that bothersome, oppressive woman who was trying with all her contrariness to slow him down and deliver him to the authorities. *Well damn her and her obstinate orneriness. She can just lie there on the wood plank floor for all I care. If she hadn't stopped for me, I wouldn't be burdened with her. This is her fault, my having to deal with her at all.* He opened a tin of Spam and wolfed it down cold.

The woodstove was heating up now, making the interior of the little cabin more pleasant, and he tossed coffee into an old-fashioned, open coffee pot and added some icy water that he had scooped up from the creek out front. Later he would make a more complete meal for himself.

I suppose I'll have to feed her something. Unless she dies before I have to, he chuckled to himself. But as he looked her over, it seemed that her extreme paleness was fading, and she was showing a little bit of color in her cheeks. *Okay,* he observed, *her heart's still beating, and circulation is improving.* Muscles were still twitching, but she didn't seem to be convulsing as before. *Guess she's going to make it, and I'll have her clean herself up and give me some fun.* But for now, she was still unconscious. He decided to remove the duct tape covering her mouth, which aided her breathing.

Damn, I'm tired. I'm going to get some shut-eye. He wrestled Crystal up into a plain, wooden, straight-back chair, one of four that clustered around the little table at one side of the main room. He took some rope and tied her ankles to the front legs of the chair, and then he tied her wrists together behind her back. Last, he ran a couple of loops of the rope around her waist and tied the ends behind the chair back. In doing so, he brushed his hands against her ample breasts. *Well, that felt kinda good,* he thought, *but I'm too damn tired. Maybe later, if she's still alive,* he chortled.

She still hadn't regained consciousness, and her breathing was ragged and struggling. She still felt cold to the touch, despite the warming interior of the cabin. He left her slumped forward in the chair near the center of the room. He didn't bother replacing the tape. If she woke up and started getting noisy, he'd hear it immediately – even in his slumber – and shut her up right fast. Maybe even forever. He really hadn't decided about that yet.

He looked to the two small bedrooms in the back of the cabin. There was no bath nor inside toilet. The creek was for bathing, and outside, a few yards to the side of the cabin was the decrepit, old outhouse – a "one-holer" at that. One of the bedrooms was unusable. The old, plank roof having collapsed inward, with sand, moss, and woody debris spilling into the room. But he didn't care. He just kept that bedroom door closed, latched shut actually, with a clamp. Sure, deer mice and other critters got in there at will. Once a porcupine that gnawed around at the interior sides of the logs. But anyone who accidentally stumbled across the old cabin would see that a back corner of the roof had caved in, and it made it look that much more abandoned and unoccupied.

It was perfect, for that matter. It was very unlikely that anyone would come there, and even if they just happened to, you could pass right by on the higher ground and not even see the little structure, tucked back into the bank rising up from the creek bottom. It couldn't be spotted from the air, despite the fact that the state police would surely send a chopper or two up to search for him. The little cedar swamp creek was too small and too tangled with thick cedar trees and downed logs for any wading fisherman to pass by. Let alone any small canoe or other craft.

Nonetheless, he had carefully placed warning traps all around the outside of the cabin. On the overgrown path coming down from high ground he had placed well-hidden cords with tin cans dangling unseen in the thicker brush on each side of the path. He had tested them, and they made a real racket if someone tripped on the cord. Along the edge of the gurgling creek a few yards on either side of the cabin – both upstream and downstream – he had constructed large deadfalls. He chose the only spots where someone could squeeze through the thick, interlocking cedar trees to approach the cabin, and had propped up large, heavy logs that blended perfectly with the surrounding trees.

In a clever and effective use of leverage, the logs both up- and down-stream were kept in place by sturdy, smaller sticks, with virtually invisible "trigger sticks" fastened to them and poking out into the spots allowing passage of a person. When someone ducked through the opening, they couldn't avoid running into the trigger stick, which would collapse the support stick, instantly sending the big log down on the head of the intruder.

Such deadfalls were crude but effective traps for all manner of furbearing animals, up to and including full-grown bears. Having one drop on a person's head would almost always be fatal, and even if the victim escaped death, the chances of a broken back, shoulder, or leg were really high. On rare occasion, someone might have such quick and lucky reflexes as to fall back and avoid the deadfall log, but at an absolute minimum the noise of the falling log would alert him in the cabin a few yards away.

His warning system and traps were rustic, he readily admitted, but he was extremely skilled at such woods-craft devices, and his success rate was excellent with all kinds of animals. And they didn't have technological failures like electronic gizmos. A meth-making friend of his had suffered the loss of his lab last year when his trail camera and motion sensor failed and didn't detect a narcotics team approaching his place. He had no way of knowing, nor would he care, of course, that it had been the first raid that Officer Andrea Henriks had participated in.

The second bedroom was still intact and solid, including the roof above the ceiling, and he went in and flopped on one of the two cots there. Sleep came quickly and deeply. But he had always had the ability to awaken at the slightest sound or disturbance. As he drifted off, he thought *my brother will hear on the news of the cops finding the dead trooper, and he'll get over here when he thinks it's safe. I'll wait until he shows up, and then we can decide what to do with this damned woman.*

CHAPTER TEN

A few hours later, when it was approaching noon that Saturday morning, he woke and felt refreshed. He went out into the main room, and though Crystal was still slumped over, her color was much better, just about back to normal. He checked the ropes. No sign that she had awakened while he was dozing and tried to wriggle free. Besides, his knots were perfect. He decided to venture outside and have a look around, so precaution dictated that he replace the tape over her mouth. *There, that'll keep her quiet.* Crystal muttered incomprehensibly at being taped again but didn't really become conscious.

He put the hip boots on, took a small spinning rod with him, went down to the creek just in front of the cabin, and started flipping a spinning lure under partially submerged cedar logs.

Before long, a solid strike occurred and he hoisted out a fat, beautifully colored, native brook trout. It was only about 8-9 inches long, but in this small stream they seldom grew to much more than 10 inches. It didn't matter, at any size they were delicious coated with flour, salt and pepper and fried in the Crisco oil he kept in the cache. He worked his way downstream a short way, continuing to flip little casts alongside and under logs, and soon he had a half-dozen brookies. A couple were only about 7 inches, but still big enough to eat. He walked back to the cabin and behind it to the cache.

The cache was like an old-fashioned root cellar – a small cave carved into the sloping bank that the cabin butted up against in the back. He had expertly lined the walls and ceiling with small logs carefully fitted together to prevent cave-ins, and made a small door out of rough planks that fit snugly in a plank door frame. The door opening was less than four feet high, requiring him to stoop low to enter, but inside the ceiling rose up to almost five feet above the dirt floor, so that he could straighten up a little bit more, but still be hunched over.

He had a latch with a padlock that was like the one on the cabin door. It didn't require a key, since like the cabin lock, all he had to do was strike the lock sharply with a heavy metal bar and it would fall open. That way, there was no need to remember keys, and to anyone who would somehow discover the place, it looked for all the world as though it was solidly locked up.

The cache was subterranean except at the little door, so the cool temperatures of the earth down in the creek bed kept it like a refrigerator – or, again, an old-fashioned root cellar – and it was where he stored anything that might be perishable, including some rib cages and haunches from deer he had poached with his favorite crossbow. He also had some small wooden boxes with potatoes, onions and carrots, and occasionally he would stick a jug of milk or cider in there to keep cool. If Northern Michigan got unusually hot in July and August, he could tote a block of ice in and keep the cache colder.

But particularly now in late October the cache kept whatever was placed inside at a 40-some degree temperature, and part of the beauty of his primitive arrangement was that it also wouldn't drop much below 40 even in January when the outside temperature might be well below zero. He didn't need the uncertainty, expense, or attention that electrical service would have involved. He hanged two of the larger, gutted trout on a forked stick attached to the plank ceiling of the cache. He would fry up four of them for his lunch and catch some more for a meal tomorrow or Monday. Supper would be a thick steak of the dried venison cut off one of the deer haunches in the cache. His mouth watered at the thought of eating these products of Nature's bounty that he had harvested. Trout fishing in inland streams was officially over for the year at the end of September, but he paid no attention to the Michigan state game laws and seasons. They were artificial, nonsensical, and had nothing to do with proper living off the land.

The woman, he suddenly remembered. *I suppose I'll have to feed her something. Well, she doesn't deserve these freshly caught trout. She can gnaw on some of this salt pork I have hanging here...maybe some canned red beans if she finally shows me some respect and gratitude for my putting up with her. I wonder if she's come to yet.*

He returned to the cabin and saw that she had. At least she was conscious, though dazed with blurry vision both from the concussion she had received when he first grabbed her by the stuck truck, and from the immense stress of her ordeal when being pushed and dragged through creeks and swamps for hours the previous night.

"Well, look at the lazy bones finally waking up at this late hour," he mocked her. Crystal struggled to clear her throat and form some words.

"Why...why did you bring me here? What do you want from me? Is it...is it money? Take what I have in my purse. It's yours. Where is my purse? Where are we? Oh, God, I'm so cold and it hurts so bad." And she couldn't keep talking without bursting into tears and shivering again.

Damn. Women are such a bother. Always complaining and nagging and crying and making me miserable. From my mom to that bitch who divorced me, always on my back about every little thing. It's much better when they're on their backs, he chuckled to himself. *Speaking of that, I should give her a wash rag and some soap and water so's she can clean herself up. Who wants to take that sorry mess to bed?*

"Here," he barked at Crystal, "wash that muck off yourself." And he set down the wash pan and some soap and a tattered, old wash cloth. "Now I'm going to untie you so's you can clean yourself off, but don't get any funny ideas about trying to run off or scream or make a fuss. Nobody's around for miles in this forest, but I still don't want to hear you so much as peep"

He loosened the ropes, but without warning he slapped her across the mouth with the back of his rough hand, shocking her to a more alert state, her eyes wide and greatly afraid.

"You hear me? You better behave or a lot worse will come upon your sorry ass. Not so much as a flinch, you understand?" he growled.

Crystal kept her head down but nodded fearfully, forcing herself to be as quiet as she could manage, while continuing to shiver...now as much from fear as from her being chilled to her bones.

"Now clean yourself up, and I'll fix a plate for you, much as I hate having you eat my food."

She was afraid to say much or ask for anything, but the smell of the coffee he had boiled was too much to resist. As much as she didn't want to give him any reason to strike her again or inflict any other additional abuse, she worked up the courage to ask in a small, shaky voice,   "Could I have some of that hot coffee, please? I'll stay right here and not make any trouble for you," she added. "Please?"

Damn women, always wanting and wanting. Something's never enough with bitches. He scowled but decided that maybe a cup of coffee would give her something to sip and shut her up, stop bothering him. *Why do I have to be burdened with her? It's not fair.* But he poured the coffee into an old restaurant mug with a cracked rim and handed it to her roughly.

"Here. Now quit yer moaning and don't keep bothering me."

The coffee was strong and very hot, but maybe never had a sip of coffee felt so good to Crystal. The almost-burning liquid went down her throat to her frozen core and instantly she felt ever so slightly better. It was somehow the first tiny sliver of hope she had received. Although at that point she couldn't imagine any other source of hope. Nobody knew where she was, who had taken her, or if she was still alive.

Her thinking gradually improved beyond sheer panic, terror, and despair. She knew from her self-defense classes that she needed to try to make some connection with her brutal captor, to somehow make him see her as a person like himself, not just an undesirable object. He obviously didn't want to have to talk to her or interact with her more than he felt he had to, but she had to find the smallest cracks in his psychological armor to make that personal connection. She tried to focus on him, what mattered to him, when and how she could slip in a comment or question that wouldn't infuriate him or propel him into violence toward her. She was greatly anxious, of course, that he would move on to brutal sexual assault. She didn't want to contemplate that scenario, but as much as she wanted to reject the thought, she knew enough that if it came to that, she would have to find the strength to endure it. Resistance and trying to fight him off would almost certainly result in severe injury, maybe even death. And Crystal didn't want to die.

All these thoughts milled around in her aching head as she took more sips of the spirit-bolstering coffee. She looked down with some disdain at the salt pork and hardtack he had put on an aluminum plate at her feet. But two important facts she drew from the disgusting fare:

First, she needed to eat whatever she could for her own strength and energy, including trying to restore her core body temperature.

And second, however much he viewed her with contempt, at least he was giving her food and drink. He could have just killed her outright and left her to rot in one of those horrible swamps. Whatever he really wanted from her, he was keeping her alive...for now, at least.

The combination of the hot coffee, giving herself a sponge bath with the basin of heated water, and the room warmed by the wood stove, actually helped to relax her somewhat and make her sleepy...especially since she was still tremendously fatigued by the whole ordeal he had put her through. Her head slumped again as she sat on the chair she had been bound to, and she nodded off.

Meanwhile, he had fried up his freshly caught trout, prepared himself a heaping mound of sliced potatoes and onions, and complemented his feast with hot, hard cider. By the time he finished, it occurred to him that Crystal had been even more quiet than usual, and when he bothered to look, saw that she had nodded off in the chair in the center of the room. He also noticed that she had managed to wash off most of the mud and black muck on her legs and arms. Her clothes were a dirty mess, but she looked better...although her long, dark hair was tangled and needed a thorough shampooing and brushing.

He thought about having her remove those torn and dirty clothes and join him in the bedroom, but now with a full belly and warmed by the woodstove, he found that he, too, was feeling drowsy.

Ah, let her be. She'd just make a fuss and I'd have to subdue her to have my way with her. We'll be here for a while. There's plenty of time to bang her later. He locked the one door to the cabin so that it couldn't be opened from either side and went back to the bedroom to lie down. His outside alarm system would wake him from light sleep in the unlikely event that anyone would approach.

CHAPTER ELEVEN

When he woke later in the afternoon, he shuffled back out to the main room and was amused that Crystal had slid off of the chair seat and was curled in a fetal position on the plank floor, still sound asleep. He decided to go out and check his trap line in the swamp. Trapping of wild animals that inhabited the cedar swamp and creek – like mink, raccoons, otter, foxes, bobcat, coyotes, and farther downstream where the creek was wider, beaver – was also not open yet for the state trapping season, but neither did he care about those restrictions that the damned government tried to impose. As soon as he judged that the fur-bearing animals were growing their thicker fur for the fall/winter season, he put out his traps. It was a cash crop for him, and important in being able to live off the land.

Disciplined and detailed about his trapping, as he was in all of his formidable wood craft, he checked the line daily to harvest any and all kills as quickly as possible. The last thing he wanted was for scavengers to ruin the furs by tearing at the dead animal in the trap. He would have checked at first light that morning had he not been forced to nursemaid that infernal, whining woman. It took the better part of two hours to go up and down both sides of the creek near the cabin, checking his traps, removing any catch, dispatching wounded animals, rebaiting and resetting the traps. But he loved being the dominant predator...in any environment.

It was nearing suppertime when he got back to the cabin with his take of two dark-furred mink, one hefty boar raccoon, and a snowshoe hare that had been in transition from its summer brown fur to the all-white that would camouflage it so effectively in the deep snows of winter. The lush, dark-brown mink would fetch a good price at the fur shows, as would the nearly perfect pelt of the big raccoon. The swamp rabbit wasn't worth much, but after skinning, fleshing, stretching, salting, drying and tanning the skin, the mottled brown and white would make a nice trim for mittens or a hat. It was fair production for the last two days.

Cash for his furs stirred his thinking about the much more lucrative drug business he was involved in. He had not forgotten, of course, the meth he had safeguarded in his knapsack over the last 24 hours. He didn't like the cooking or any other aspect of the production of the methamphetamine – his older brother took care of that – but he had become the regular distributor to their markets in the larger cities downstate, like Grand Rapids, Big Rapids, Mt. Pleasant, Midland, and the Saginaw/Bay City area. It was a typical middle-of-the-night delivery run that the stupid state trooper had interrupted along Highway 72 west of Kalkaska.

He was also very disciplined and detailed about the drug business, which is why he was entrusted to make the deliveries and collect the money from mid-level distributors and dealers. Big brother and a couple of his ne'er-do-well, usually between jobs, friends who were involved in the meth production also liked the fact that he took neither lip nor any crap from anyone. No one tried to rip him off or cheat on a deal, because the trooper wasn't the only one who had ever felt the steel of one of his Bowie knives. Mostly a nasty slash to an arm or leg and wrestling the thug to the ground, threatening worse with the knife, had been more than sufficient deterrent, but once he had fatally slashed the throat of an inner-city gang member who tried to steal his product. He was totally certain that it wasn't a loss that meant anything to anyone...most of all, himself.

As he placed the animals in the cool cache to preserve them until skinning later, he fussed to himself about the aborted drug delivery. The distributors and dealers would be wondering what happened to him that he didn't show up when expected. Their enthusiastic customers would be complaining and whining about the lack of product to buy. The party boys and girls would be bitching about no meth for their expected highs at their favorite clubs and parties. He provided an important, valuable service that was going unfilled. But worst of all, he had no thick wad of cash to hand over to his brother and his friends.

Why is this happening to me? I don't deserve the grief that stupid cop and this nasty woman have caused me. It's their fault, not mine, he reminded himself. But would big brother see it that way? Would he get blamed for their wrongs he was forced to suffer? His recently buoyant mood while cruising his trap line had swung like the proverbial pendulum over to the misery and injustice inflicted upon him during the previous night and today. He locked up the cache and strode over to the cabin, his mind set on teaching the dumb woman a harsh lesson for mistreating him. Maybe some rough sex before fixing supper. Not that she deserved any food. He had been too nice to her with that lunch he had given her.

But before he could unlock and enter the cabin door, a slight clatter of cans several yards up the overgrown path to the high ground announced the approach of an intruder. He was instantly on guard for whatever he might have to do...but also smiling, because he was absolutely certain it was his brother coming to meet him. He played a constant game with his big brother by moving his alarm trap each time after they met there at the cabin. Big brother knew that he would do that, but most of the time he couldn't detect where the new location of the trap was set up. His older brother was an experienced woodsman, but no one could match his own skill in virtually every aspect of life in the forest.

In a matter of seconds, the two were reunited and greeted each other with bear hugs.

"What happened?" his big brother wanted to know. "Our customers downstate were bitching to me on the phone that you never showed. And what are you doing here at the cabin? What's wrong?"

The two brothers had long had a contingency plan that if anything went awry with any aspect of the meth business – whether production problems, a raid by the narcotics cops on their Traverse City lab, disruption of their distribution and delivery network, suspicion of undercover drug enforcement agents, or some other serious problem – they would rendezvous by the next day at the old log cabin to lie low and decide what to do. They had found the place, obviously abandoned, unused, and starting to fall down, on one of their joint deer poaching efforts, and had decided that it was a perfect hideaway. It only took a little effort to make it satisfactory for their purposes, and little brother especially took to it as his primary residence. He just loved stalking the forest, exercising his superior outdoor skills, and being The Predator.

"Now before I let you in," the younger brother cautioned, "I have to fill you in on what happened last night. I had to take direct, corrective action...and, oh, we have a guest."

CHAPTER TWELVE

"**N**o, not a state cop," big brother exploded by the cabin door. "Oh, shit. I was afraid that was you. Why'd you have to kill him?"

"Hey, back off, bro'" his little brother grew indignant. "You think I wanted that? It was his fault, stopping me for no good reason. And I couldn't let him find the meth stash now, could I? And I lost my favorite blade, damn it. Had to leave it sticking in the pig."

Big brother would have cracked a smile at the reference to "stuck pig" if he hadn't been so distraught that he grabbed the sides of his head and tried to control his thoughts and feelings under the assault of the seriousness of the murder along the forest highway. He paced frantically back and forth a few yards each way between the cabin and the creek, trying to organize his thoughts. He had heard about the murder on the television news, of course, and had even spotted a state police helicopter in a search pattern as he cautiously made his way toward the swamp in which the cabin was hidden.

At one point, he had pulled off the heavily-shaded two-track lane into a space under tall trees when the 'copter swung closer to his line of travel. He was confident, however, that no one – especially no authorities – had observed his winding back into the depths of the swamp. The seldom-used two-track came to a dead-end at a small opening among thick aspen which was just large enough to turn around and hold at most a couple of vehicles. The trees around the little clear spot made it invisible from above until the leaves were down, and in the unlikely event that any hunter or hiker found their way into the spot, it looked for all the world as though it was a place where a hunter would park to hunt the nearby swamp. The old path had gone unused for years before the brothers detected it, and it didn't even look like a path at all until a person pushed a hundred feet or so into the woods lining the swamp. Then it looked like a deer trail, winding through the thick trees and brush until it reached the cabin spot about a hundred yards in.

Big brother hadn't really gotten his head around the murder of Trooper Baldwin when the second bit of disturbing news from his younger brother registered in his mind.

"You said 'a guest?' What guest? And why would you ever bring someone in here?"

"I didn't want to, believe me, but when I spun out into the soft, wet sand near the North Branch, hey, I needed transportation out of there before cops came," his little brother explained. "This bar bimbo came along in her dented, old Oldsmobile, and what was I going to do with her? Couldn't jack her car and leave her by the truck to give the police a description of me. I didn't want to kill her there and leave another body behind me with more evidence for them to find. I brought her along with me while I shook the fools and their tracking dogs offa my trail. She's not a bad looker.

Maybe you and I can have some fun with her while we decide what to do with her."

Big brother stood in the small space in front of the cabin door, shaking his head and running his fingers through his long, graying hair.

My baby brother may know woods stuff, but he's always been an idiot. Killing a state cop and kidnapping a woman. What's wrong with his head? Well, I better lie low here for a while myself. They're gonna be looking for me as well as him. He's right about one thing: we'll have to decide what to do with this woman. It's way bad enough for him to be a cop killer, but kidnapping and maybe multiple homicides? Maybe we can leave her where somebody would find her well after we made our escape. I don't know. I have to think on this. Well, we better dig in here for the time being.

"Come on in," little brother encouraged him. "I was just about to fix some venison for supper. And you can meet the bitch. See what you think," he smiled and winked.

"Hold on, butt-head. You better hike back up the path with me and help me pull some camo netting over my car. It's well-screened from aerial view now, but leaves are coming down every day, and soon it could be spotted if they flew right over it."

"Okay," his younger brother agreed. "But watch your step with my alarm system. You sounded like a brass band coming in here," he laughed and took a poke at big brother's shoulder.

The kid's right. I knew he had it set up somewhere along the path, but I didn't see it. He's good at that stuff. Well, we'll hide the car. I'll see about this woman he snatched. Then that venison sounds good. Maybe this evening we can come up with a plan to get outta here. Seems we've outworn our stay in Northern Michigan.

CHAPTER THIRTEEN

Crystal had been unbound and her mouth was not taped the whole time her kidnapper had been out checking his trap line. Since both the cabin door and the only window had been locked from the outside, she knew she couldn't escape, and that it would only bring his violent wrath down upon her if she hollered for help. Besides, the way he had brought her to this place deep in the swamp had convinced her that there was probably no one else anywhere nearby to be able to hear her scream.

Still, she moved freely about the little cabin, looking around thoroughly. Perhaps there was some way to break out besides going through either the door or the window. Maybe she could find and hide something for a weapon in case he assaulted her and she had to fight for her life. Warmth and food had helped her to find some small measure of hope that this nightmare ordeal would reach an end eventually...and that she'd still be alive when it did. She had always believed in the providence of God and in guardian angels, and she prayed for them now...and hoped that human searchers could somehow find her.

She looked in the rough cupboards and drawers. She knew she had to be careful not to disturb anything so that he would know she had been snooping. She had hoped she could find a sharp kitchen knife to hide for herself, but all she came across were mismatched eating utensils – butter knives, forks and spoons. *Figures,* she sniffed to herself, *he seems to cut everything with his big sheath knife.* Nonetheless, since there were probably ten or more old forks of different designs, she decided to slip one into her deep jeans pocket. He probably didn't bother to count them every time he wanted to use a fork. It wouldn't be enough of a weapon to do him, or anyone, real harm, but maybe it could break his grip and let her wrestle free at some point in the future. *I have to be able to do something if he doesn't just set me free, or if rescuers don't show up.* While she constantly feared for her life, Crystal Johnson was the kind of woman that if she was going to die, she'd rather die fighting, even if it was futile.

The door was open to the bedroom that he used and looking in she could see the two metal cots, with a small table between them like a nightstand, and a dilapidated but still functional chest of drawers with a cracked mirror hanging on the wall over it. Maybe she'd rummage through the drawers later, but again, she would have to be careful not to leave anything looking as if she had disturbed it. She went over to the other bedroom door and looked at the latch and clamp that kept it closed. She wanted to look in there, too, but knew that she would probably make some noise trying to unclamp and unlatch the door, so she went to the outside door and listened for a good, long minute. Then she did the same at the shuttered window. There was no sound outside that he had come back.

Crystal levered open the heavy clamp with a bit of a clatter, then pried open the rusty latch with the fork she had pilfered. As soon as the second bedroom door was swung open, she could smell the dank, moldy interior of the room and saw the partially collapsed ceiling and roof. There were gnawing marks on the interior logs and wooden frames around the door from rodents, as well as droppings throughout the room. A rusty old metal cot was still left in the room, but its thin mattress had been thoroughly gutted of its stuffing by nest-making rodents. Any other furniture that had been in the room at any time had been removed.

She peered upward at the caved-in ceiling and collapsed roof above it. *If animals can get in here, maybe with some effort I can work my way out,* she thought hopefully. *I'd have to wait until it seemed certain that he was going to leave me in here alone for some time.* As she slipped quietly back out of the ruined bedroom, she used a small branch with dead leaves that had fallen in through the ceiling to smooth the dirt and dust as carefully as possible on the plank floor. She didn't want any tracks she had made to alert him to the fact that she had been snooping in the unused bedroom.

She re-latched the door and replaced the heavy clamp that held the latch closed. Then she took the sleeve of her flannel shirt and wiped the floor outside the bedroom so that no tracks made by her were visible on the planks by the latched door. She felt as confident as she could that there was no sign of her having entered that abandoned bedroom or having even approached the latched door. She was going to go back to the old straight-back chair she had been bound to and sit down and wait for him to return when she finally heard noises and muffled voices outside the cabin.

What Crystal heard was the brothers squabbling on the other side of the locked cabin door. She realized that now she had another captor to contend with. She could only hope that he was more reachable than the surly backwoodsman who had kidnapped her. She heard them move off up the small path and wondered if they were both leaving for a time. She decided to sit and wait for a bit. If they returned soon, she would look as subdued and unresisting as possible so as not to arouse any suspicions that she had either snooped, or that she was looking for a way out. She looked down and checked to make sure that the stolen fork didn't make any bulge in her deep pocket. And sure enough, soon the two brothers were back and unlocked the door.

CHAPTER FOURTEEN

In contrast to the menacing man who had abducted her, this slightly older fellow was almost friendly. He gave a slight smile and commented almost casually.

"Well, who do we have here? Little brother said we have a guest. What's your name, sweetheart?"

Crystal didn't entertain any delusions that his friendly manner meant that all danger was past. *In all likelihood,* she thought quickly, *he just wants to get information from me...maybe gain a sense of who might be looking for me, and how soon they would possibly come out this way and this far into the forest.* Still, she instantly and instinctively decided to play along with him. At least, unlike her savage kidnapper, he wanted to talk to her, and she needed to connect with at least one of the two rough men.

"My name's Crystal, sir.May I ask yours?"

"Sir," the younger brother hooted. "Even clerks and tellers don't call him 'sir.' My big brother's lucky if he gets called to dinner," he laughed.

Big brother ignored him. "Oh, I think not, Crystal. When we drop you off, I'd rather not have you telling the police or anyone else my name. It's suppertime, Crystal. You're probably hungry, right? Little brother will show you where the dishes are. Why don't you set the table for the three of us? And you can help with the food. Okay?"

She could feel excitement surge inside of her at the mention of "dropping you off," but she fought any impulse to show enthusiasm. She knew full well that he could be lying about any such intent, and that he could be trying to disarm her guardedness about revealing anything about herself and who might be looking for her even now.

"Okay, I'll be glad to help."

The younger brother grimaced at having to interact with Crystal in any "normal" way, but he pushed her rather roughly toward the cupboard next to the table pushed against the wall.

"Plates over there on the right. Cups and glasses on the left. Utensils in that drawer. I'll start the venison steaks frying," he said to his brother, not to her.

Big brother suggested to Crystal that she could use a scraper in the drawer to peel carrots and potatoes in the box on the counter.

"But you better not poke anything with that scraper other than vegetables, you hear?"

Crystal nodded in the affirmative as she got plates out of the cupboard and distributed them around three sides of the table.

"Yah," younger brother agreed. "If any poking's gonna be done it'll be us poking you in the bedroom," he laughed menacingly.

Big brother didn't say anything, but he quietly shook his head slightly. *The kid's always talking about banging some woman, whether a date or some complete stranger. But he hasn't been able to get it up for years now. "Erectile dysfunction" everybody's calling it. He's tried those pills, but whatever kind, they just seem to make him flushed and anxious. His heart races. He keeps thinking that it's the woman's fault, and that if he hooks up with the right woman, or if a woman treats him right...well, it'll work again. All I know is that he always "wants" a woman, and then he's in a rage when he can't "do" her. From that bruising on her cheek, he's probably been pretty rough on this Crystal. He just gets so frustrated. And whatever upsets him, it's somebody else's fault...hell, it's everybody else's fault. Family, gotta love 'em, even if you can't stand 'em. Idiot kid.*

By the time the sun set about 6:30, the swamp and forest outside the cabin was darkening quickly. The three companions in the small, rough log cabin finished their surprisingly fine meal with occasional bits of conversation. But truth be told, not a one of them wanted to be there under the current circumstances.

The younger brother felt most at home in the wild and tucked away in this woodsman's cabin, but he relentlessly resented the imposition of this troublesome woman who had forced him to abduct her. *That stupid cop and this stupid bimbo are ruining everything for me.*

The older brother was thinking nonstop about how the two of them could get out of this murder and kidnap mess that his baby brother had gotten him into. There must be some avenue of escape. Maybe get down to West Virginia and hide out with kin in the Appalachian Mountains. But how best to do it without getting caught...and what to do with this Crystal? He really didn't want to have to kill her, but what were the chances they could leave her alive and not have her sic the authorities on their trail before getting hidden away in some Seneca Rocks hollow in the

Appalachians? *Well, tomorrow's Sunday. We might as well hole up here until the beginning of next week. By Monday I'll have a plan...and I'll have figured out what to do with Crystal. Not a bad-looking girl. Shame she was in the wrong place at the wrong time. Oh, well. Shit happens.*

"Crystal, why don't you wash up our dishes in the basin of water over on the counter below the cupboard? The kettle on the wood stove is full of hot water, and the cupboard under the silverware drawer has dish soap. The drawer alongside the silverware has a couple of dish towels. Little brother and I are gonna play some cards here as soon as you get these dishes off our 'card table.'" He laughed, but she rightly understood it to be a command, not a request. Big brother was treating her more kindly, and the meal was the most she had had since earlier on Friday, but she had no delusions about any goodness in his heart. If he felt he had to, he would probably kill her just about as quickly as his little brother would, although just maybe he wouldn't do it so casually or so brutally.

As she was washing and drying their dishes, a curious thought crept into her mind. *Despite all his references to forcing sex upon me, why hasn't the younger one done anything about it? And why, if he doesn't want to force me, does he keep making cracks about it as though he will? And why do they not use names for each other? "Little brother," and "My big brother." Is it just that they are thinking about letting me go at some point and they don't want me to have names to pass on to the police, like the older one said?*

Crystal finished with the dishes and frying pans and kept glancing over at their rather noisy game of cribbage. As it got later, she did worry about whether either one or both were going to force her onto one of the cots. She decided not to think about that definite possibility. But the thought of the cots made her wonder: obviously the two brothers were going to sleep in the two cots in the bedroom. What would they do with her? She hoped they wouldn't tie her up in the rough straight chair and tape her mouth again for the night. She would plead for them not to if it looked like they might. After all, they locked the door and the window against going out or coming in, so she couldn't very well go anywhere.

She sat down quietly and tried to be as invisible as she could be by remaining motionless and not saying anything. A second game was followed by a third as the two of them taunted each other in their spirited play, which was augmented by a whiskey bottle and glasses that they had brought out from a lower cupboard.

While they argued genially about whether to play yet a fourth game – it had been a long, arduous night the night before, and the younger brother had to be tired from all the activity – Crystal decided to roll up the dry towel from her earlier sponge bath, tiptoed quietly over to a corner, and laid down, using the towel as a pillow. She slipped the fork out of her jeans pocket unseen and hid it under some old newspapers that were piled up in a careless stack. It wouldn't be good to have it detected in her pocket if one or both of them decided to "feel her up." She had no blanket, but the wood stove kept the little cabin toasty warm, and she curled up and soon fell asleep with her exhaustion. The brothers hardly took note of her, so long as she was quiet and didn't bother them.

"Oh, look, your little 'guest' has dozed off over there on the floor," big brother chuckled.

"She's not mine," the younger brother objected. "And if we're not going to put her on her back in the bedroom, maybe I should haul her sorry ass up and out to the cache. I can lock her up in there for the night, maybe then she won't trouble us."

"Oh, leave her be. We can deal with her in the morning.

Besides, it wasn't so bad to have a dishwasher, was it? Let's turn in. You don't have any of your weapons where she can reach them, do you?"

"You think I'm nuts? You know I keep my Bowie with me at all times. Good thing I had my back-up blade when I had to leave 'number one' in the stupid cop. I keep my crossbow locked up in that corner cupboard...until I need to harvest some fresh venison, of course. My whittling and fish-cleaning knife is always in my pocket. So, no. Ain't any weapons she can reach."

"What about sharp kitchen knives?"

"Nope, just butter knives. You know I cut everything with my Bowie, don't need no kitchen blades. You need to have more confidence in me, big brother. There ain't no way the little bimbo's gonna get the drop on me. Maybe you, you softy, but not me." He leaned over and gave a playful punch to his brother's shoulder. He lifted the coffee pot from the wood stove and drained the last bit of liquid, filling his cup only halfway.

The older brother reflected on the kid's inventory of weapons. *He's always liked knives and things with sharp blades. Never took to guns. Years ago, when he was still in his early teens, I remember him saying that guns were for the unskilled, for poor woodsmen and soft city slickers. He figured that he could learn to stalk deer and other critters as well as the old Injuns. And by this point, he can. Never seen anybody who could stalk and become so motionless that he could reach out and touch a deer as it stepped by on a trail.*

He'd probably be a purist and insist on using an old-fashioned Injun bow to make the hunt fair, but he likes the firepower of the crossbow. Told me once that if he ever squeezed down a swamp trail and came nose-to-nose with an angry bear, he wanted his PSE TAC 15i crossbow and its better than 400 foot-pounds of target-stopping energy. "It'll stop them game wardens, too," *he used to brag. Shoot, what was it he used to boast about? Oh, yeah, that with his deadly crossbow he was Death stalking in the forest.*

"I seen you were using the cot on the left, so I'll take the one to the right. Good night, baby brother."

The younger brother waved him good night and sipped on the last of the coffee. As soon as he drained the cup, he got up, turned off the little lantern and glanced over at Crystal sound asleep in the corner. *Cooking and dishwashing aside, maybe I should have left her body in the swamp. We can still have some fun with her, though. If I was really a good brother, maybe I should let him have first crack at her. Sleep tight, bitch. In that corner bed bugs and all sorts of nasties might just bite.* He laughed to himself at his little joke and went to bed.

CHAPTER FIFTEEN

Sunday morning shortly before sunup the younger brother unlocked the cabin door and went out to check his trap line. His older brother got up to have coffee with him, but he would wait until he returned a couple of hours later to have bacon, eggs, and toast. They let Crystal continue to sleep in her curled-up position in the corner.

At about the same time, Officer Andrea Henriks went into her Traverse City Post early. She pulled out files for the Traverse Narcotics Team meeting that would convene at 9:00 A.M. on Monday. The search was continuing through the weekend and round-the-clock to the east for Trooper Baldwin's killer, and the State Police Helicopter and the dog handlers on the ground continued to spiral the search grid outward from the scene of the stuck truck on Sharon Road. Once her TNT members went over all the known and suspected drug houses or makeshift labs in that meeting, they would plan and coordinate raids for that coming week throughout the Grand Traverse area. Somewhere they would find someone who knew the unknown suspect who was transporting the meth when Trooper Baldwin was murdered.

The actual raids would commence on Thursday, which would see a significant increase in person power and resources of every kind applied to the manhunt. Federal Bureau of Investigation agents would be arriving to advise and lend expertise since there was now a kidnapping involved. Drug Enforcement Agency agents would also be coming to broaden the resources and add to the number of investigators available to work the narcotics side of the case. Since plans would be held in readiness until the Feds arrived, the TNT lead officer told Andrea to go ahead with her Wednesday afternoon off, but to report early and be ready to go on Thursday morning.

Late Sunday afternoon the brothers decided to lock Crystal up in the cabin while they did some scouting of the area for about a mile in radius. They needed to know if the police search had shifted farther west in their direction. They had no way of knowing, of course, that at just that time the Kalkaska County Sheriff deputy was checking out the rusty, old, red pickup truck stuck in the wet, sandy ditch near the North Branch of the Manistee. There was no vehicle movement anywhere near the cabin, and not even a bird hunter or a bow hunter to be seen in the surrounding forest for hundreds of yards, so they slipped back to the cabin for supper and another evening of card-playing.

As they hiked back through pathless woods, they debated just how and when to make their escape and try to head down to West Virginia. It would help greatly if they had indications that the manhunt had shifted farther away from them. The topic of Crystal and her fate had been set aside for the time being. The priority was getting out of Northern Michigan without being caught. Big brother hadn't told anyone where he was headed when he had driven out of

Traverse City early Saturday evening. And he hadn't stopped for gas or anything else, so there should be no witness to give a statement about his activity back then. Little brother was almost always in this cabin deep in the swamp, having only gone into Traverse City to pick up the meth delivery late Friday night.

When they unlocked the cabin and went in, they were both surprised to find that Crystal had set the table for the three of them and had baked some biscuits with the baking mix she found in the cupboard and the milk that had been left out of the cache from lunch time.

"Fresh-baked biscuits, eh?" the older brother said casually, but with the slightest hint of appreciation. His younger brother just sniffed, "Trying to get on our good side, bitch? We're still putting you on your backside one of these times."

Yeah? Crystal thought without expression. *Then why haven't you made a move yet, jerk?* But she buried that feeling and just smiled. "I would have started frying the trout for you, but I guess they're out in the root cellar?"

"It's called a 'cache,' bimbo," younger brother corrected her. But she smiled inwardly, *At least you're bothering to talk to me. Before you probably wouldn't have cared what I called it.* It was still her fervent hope that she could interact with both of them and get the younger one in particular to see her as a person, rather than prey to be killed.

"She's right, kiddo. Why don't you go get those fish? And, I'll get the skillet hot."

The mean one probably didn't like that, Crystal thought, *big brother making it sound like he was siding with me, but maybe I can work with that.*

"Oh, I'm glad to get the skillet and start melting the Crisco, if you would please get those beautiful trout you caught. You must be a really good fisherman."

She hoped she wasn't overplaying the praise, but younger brother seemed to lap it up...maybe because he was always trying to prove something to his big brother.

"You're damned right I am. I catch 'em when nobody else can. I'll be right back."

Now she had both of them communicating with her. The faint sparks of hope flared ever so slightly brighter in her mind and heart. The trout supper with more potatoes and onions turned out to be delicious, and the brothers couldn't help themselves from enjoying the hot biscuits, made even better with butter and some honey that Crystal had found in the back of an upper cupboard.

"Damn good biscuits, little girl," the older one went so far as to praise her.

"I guess they're okay...but I still like them rolled the way Mom used to," the younger one added.

Still, not too bad, coming from him, Crystal felt. *If we're making progress here, I just pray God keeps me moving to their good sides...if they truly have good sides. Anything, just so they don't decide I'm too much of a liability to keep alive.*

The brothers brought out the cribbage board and cards for their evening games by the light of the small lantern. Crystal decided to push a little harder in trying to establish some good will with them.

"I see that you can play three-handed with that board," she observed. "My daddy taught me how to play, although I understand if you wouldn't want a girl beating you." She bit her lower lip slightly, fervently hoping she hadn't pushed too far.

"As if that's gonna happen," the younger, meaner one retorted. "Anyway, this is a private game, invitation only," he sneered.

Big brother, like most older brothers, enjoyed needling

his sibling. "You're not afraid of playing cards with a girl, are you? Maybe we should see what she can do. Deal her in."

Little brother grumbled about it, cursing under his breath, but he dutifully dealt out three hands to start the game. Crystal played skillfully, but kept her comments restrained while the brothers hooted and hollered whenever one or the other had a good hand or made a sharp play. It would not be good to brag about her successes to their detriment. Finally, on the home stretch, big brother was lagging behind, younger brother's pegs were in the lead, poised to go out, and Crystal could win the game with 15 points since she would count her hand first.

The young one dealt the cards, and Crystal's six cards included two eights, a seven, and a six. If she kept this "double run," and the cut card turned out to be an eight, a seven, or a six, she would have a minimum of 20 points. She deliberately discarded one of her eights into the crib. The cut card turned out to be another six, but because of her "ruining" her double run, her point total at the end of the hand turned out to be only 10, four points short of victory since she had scored one point during the plays they made with their cards. Older brother counted up next and his lead peg only went as far as two points shy of the "skunk corner." Younger brother counted a double run of eight and went out, past the victory total of 121, without needing to bother counting the points in the crib.

"Yahoo, brother, you stink. Woo-ee, what a stink. I told you no girl would beat me. I'm getting me a victory beer. Ha-ha."

"Good playing, mister," Crystal smiled as he rose and headed out of the cabin to get beers from the cache. "May I go, too, and use the outhouse?"

"Yah, okay, but remember, I'll be right outside, waiting for you to come out."

The two of them left the cabin together and walked a few yards to the outhouse off to the side. The cache was not far away, dug into that slope against which the cabin was built.

Out of idle curiosity, once they were outside, the older brother picked up the four cards that were laying face-down in the crib. The bottom one had been dealt from the deck. The top one had been discarded into the crib by the girl. It was an eight of clubs. *She broke up a double run in her dealt hand. Had she kept both eights, she would have had 20 points, more than enough to go out and win the game. Huh,* he pondered her strange play.

At first, he gave a little chuckle, *she let the kid win. You want a boy to like you? You let him win the game.* But then his thoughts turned much darker. For the first time he doubted his sympathy for the kidnapped young woman. *She actually played both of us. She wanted to lose. To encourage us to relax, to ease up on our watchfulness? To make us think she wasn't a threat? What's her real play here...what's she up to?* The fact that she cheated against herself made him suspicious. *You may just require heightened vigilance on our part, little lady.*

When younger brother and Crystal returned from outside, he was still overly hyped.

"God almighty, it stinks in here. Oh, 'cause you, big brother, just got skunked. And the bitch lost, too."

Crystal totally ignored his constant derision of her.

"Well, I wish I knew how to play like you, sir. I'm really tired. Okay if I lie down in my corner?"

"Go on, get out of the way. The big boys are going to play another one. That's if your stinky ass is up for another whipping, brother."

Crystal went over to the corner of the cabin where she had slept the night before. But this time some old burlap gunny sacks had been tossed over there for her to lie down on, and big brother had dug out an old, wool, Army surplus blanket for her to use. She still relied on her rolled-up towel for a pillow. It wasn't much better than the hard, bare floor, but at least it eliminated the drafts that crept across the floor.

Being the loser, big brother dealt out cards for another game for the two of them, but he glanced from time to time at Crystal, curled up, soon fast asleep. Maybe she wasn't so frightened and helpless as he had thought. He'd sleep with one eye open...and make sure that she didn't have access to anything that might be used as a weapon against them.

What's your plan, Missy?

CHAPTER SIXTEEN

Monday morning little brother left the cabin early again to check his traps. After he returned for another big breakfast, big brother suggested that the two of them go for a walk. They locked Crystal in the cabin as usual, and then picked their way up the slope to higher ground.

Nothing was said about Crystal throwing the cribbage game the night before. The kid would be enraged to think that anyone would let him win and might feel like turning violent toward the young woman. In any case, the older brother didn't want to have to deal with any messier situation just at that time. He would maintain a closer watch himself and make sure that Crystal wasn't going to try anything funny.

"Hey, Junior, I think we need to do a little recon and see if we can find out what the cops are doing in their search for you. For one thing, sooner or later they're going to broaden the search in this direction, especially since the more logical directions aren't going to pan out for them. So, we can't just stay here forever. For another thing, I've been mulling this over, and I think we'll need to be on our way to West Virginia by Wednesday night."

"But, Smitty, why wait until then?" Junior asked.

"We have things to do if we're going to get away cleanly. First, we need to pack up the stuff we really need to take with us – including the knapsack with the meth, that's our bankroll – and food to eat on the road. It's too risky to be stopping at diners and such. Someone might identify one or both of us from newscasts. We need to get rid of anything in the cabin that could possibly identify us. We'll spend a good part of Wednesday wiping away any prints or small traces of evidence that we were there, including brushing away any tracks as we're leaving."

"Shoot, why don't we just burn the place down just before we leave?"

"And send a smoke signal for anyone to see for miles around? I don't think so. Now pay attention: plan on having your breakfast tomorrow before going out on your trap line. While the girl cleans up and does the dishes, I'll go with you, and we'll pull all the traps. It might take two trips, I figure, but we'll pack them all back and store them in the cache. When any investigators come by, it'll look like this is just some old trapper's cabin, and whoever it is was here getting ready for the upcoming trapping season."

"What about my furs I got so far, and the hanging venison?"

"The furs we can pack in the car up here – that'll be some more income for us when we get to West Virginia – but except for the dried venison and jerky, just take the ribs and haunches downstream a ways in the swamp. The bobcats, foxes and coyotes will love it."

"Man, that sucks, wasting good wild meat like that," younger brother whined.

"Don't sweat it. They got deer in the Appalachians, too, you know. Now tomorrow afternoon we'll bury back in the swamp any personal stuff we don't need to take with us, especially anything that might hold some DNA. You know, like your extra hairbrush or toothbrush that you don't take when traveling. We'll have to wash and sterilize all cups, glasses and plates and bowls. We want it to look like the place is used by that anonymous trapper, but not have any of our prints left on anything. This will take longer than you might think, 'cause we need to look over everything again and again to make sure we've accounted for anything that might tell 'em we were here. Oh, and you'll have to take down your 'warning system.'"

"Okay, but I'll leave it up for tomorrow night. Take it down Wednesday just before we leave. I'll leave the deadfall traps, however," he chortled, "one or both might make a nice welcome if the pigs come snorting around." He paused for a second before moving on in their planning. "What about the stupid woman? Whatta ya gonna do with her?"

"Well, I been thinking," the older brother smiled ominously, "that maybe you're right, baby brother. Maybe, before we leave, we should have some fun with her. She's a little chunky, but still, a nice rack and ass. But hold off making a move on her until Wednesday, later in the day. If it gets messy with her, we don't want to have to clean that up, too. We can do her up here at the car before we hit the road. Be nice and relaxing for beginning our trip."

"But what do we do with her, then?" the younger brother pressed, not having gotten an answer to his question regarding Crystal's fate.

"I haven't quite decided on that one. I'd consider tying and taping her and leaving her somewhere, but damn, she knows an awful lot about us by now, right down to how to fool us at cribbage," he snickered and shook his head. As his kid brother looked perplexed, he went on. "We might just have to kill her and dispose of the body on the way south. Maybe dump her in Hopkins Creek before we skirt by Lake City. Let the current take her downstream toward the Big Manistee. We'll keep to back, secondary roads as long as possible into downstate. It's best if we stay away from towns and any major routes."

Not that he would admit it right out, but younger brother Junior was impressed. He knew he was the superior woodsman – nobody better in the forest – but big brother Smitty was always more the thinker. He planned out everything to the last degree.

"How 'bout right now we do a little scouting around here again, see if we spot anyone working our way," kid brother suggested, "then this afternoon after lunch I'll sweep out farther. I can stick to the swamp, the creek, only move up to higher ground well away from here. I'll wear my hip boots, and any tracking dogs won't pick up scent from the rubber. I'll sneak back toward South Sharon and watch for a while, see what official vehicles might be cruising up and down. They'll never know I'm around."

Smitty knew he was right. If anyone could stalk the forest undetected, it was his little brother. "Don't go any farther, though," he ordered. "They're probably still combing the Big Cannon area. And don't hide in some dense thicket and try to 'count coup' on some bloodhound or handler going by," referring to the kid's legendary touch on a passing deer. "Oh, and be sure to watch out for their 'eyes in the sky.' With leaves coming down every day, more on the ground becomes visible from those 'copters. That's a big reason I don't want to wait any longer than Wednesday night to hit the road. The aspens over there my car is hidden in still have a lot of leaves hangin' on, but before long from up above it will look like a suspicious lump of camo on the forest floor."

The two took off, keeping to thick trees and brush, and made a circle of a few hundred yards around the vicinity of the cabin. No one was to be seen, not even a bird hunter or a bow hunter out for deer. They watched over a large, open field for a good hour or so, but didn't see the State Police helicopter fly over. Everything was quiet, but was it *too* quiet?

Back at the cabin the brothers had lunch that Crystal had prepared for them – hot venison sandwiches smothered in gravy. She was determined to be useful to them, and Smitty continued to glance at her and wonder just what her plan of action was. He decided that he would stay close to the cabin for the afternoon while Junior made his long reconnaissance. In fact, maybe when she next used the outhouse, he should do a quick search of the small cabin, especially over in Crystal's little corner, and see if she had hidden away anything like a makeshift weapon to use against them.

Junior took off, and sure enough, Crystal asked to use the outhouse. Smitty walked her out there, and as soon as she entered, shut and latched the door so that she couldn't get out again.

"Hey, what...why'd you do that?" she called out as she rattled the door from the inside.

"I have something to do, just sit and read awhile," he answered. *Maybe she'll enjoy the couple of old Hunters & Trappers magazines Junior left in there*, he snickered to himself. He went back in the cabin, looked around thoroughly, and particularly tossed the blanket, towel, burlap bags and stacked-up old newspapers in Crystal's corner.

Nope, nothing she hid anywhere. He didn't know, of course, that each morning when she got up, she slipped the pilfered fork back in the deep pocket of her jeans.

Each of them was in a kind of waiting game, neither one knowing just what or when something was going to happen to change their situation. Would she make some move to attack or try to escape that would force him to dispense with her before Wednesday evening? Would Junior and he make some violent move toward her, whether to assault her in the bedroom or get rid of her permanently? Crystal accepted the fact that at any time they could decide that she had outlived what small usefulness she served.

CHAPTER SEVENTEEN

Junior proceeded just as he said he would. He hiked generally south through the swamp until he reached Little Cannon Creek, and then he picked his way carefully upstream through dense cedar tangles until he worked his way deep into Little Cannon Creek Swamp. It was basically the reverse of the route he had taken, dragging Crystal along with him, when he had torched and left her old Oldsmobile back in on the two-track lane near Big Cannon Creek. It was a lot easier going for him, however, since he didn't have to deal with her and her obstinate resistance.

He stopped well short of Fletcher Road on a thickly wooded little hill and settled down to recon for a while. He had chosen well, and by sitting in one place he could just barely make out when a police vehicle would pass on Fletcher Road. Then by moving a short distance he could also look back and see if any search vehicle went up or down South Sharon Road.

He was fully hidden by his hat-to-boots camouflage hunting clothes. Even his powerful crossbow was painted in camo design. He was invisible and undetectable. That was why he was totally shocked when, after about an hour of watching for search activity, he heard scuffling noise coming toward him through the fallen leaves and the brown, dead bracken ferns. He craned his neck to see what it was – *probably just a deer* – and waited silent and motionless for the intruder to appear.

Finally, he saw movement in the dead ferns and heard snuffling noises. He recognized the source immediately. A tracking dog had stumbled across his faint, barely discernible trail, and was hunting him down. The scent was so slight that the dog hadn't stopped to howl an announcement yet, "I've found something here, come running!" But Junior knew that the dog would cut loose at any moment. And it would have its handler with it, probably holding a long leash, and maybe one or more other officers to back them up.

There wasn't time for him to slip away undetected. There was only one thing to do. In a small opening about 30 yards away the dog stopped sniffing and raised its muzzle as if to let go with that dreaded howl, but a deadly crossbow arrow buried itself deeply in the dog's chest, bringing it down without a sound. As the dead dog kicked reflexively in the leaves and downed ferns, its handler stepped forward, still holding the leash, to see what was wrong with his poor dog.

A second arrow sped across the opening and struck the officer in the chest, toppling him backwards into the brush. Junior's aim had been expert. The arrow nicked the officer's heart, and then plowed on into his spine. He laid a couple of yards behind the dog, blood oozing around the feathered shaft stuck in his chest.

The Angel of Death swooped down, gathered up the exiting soul of the Michigan State Police dog handler, and then did something that many humans would have trouble believing. The officer's dog would be with him in the eternity of the Heavenly Kingdom. The eternal reign of God in Heaven is perfect in every respect. And no great love is excluded...all is perfected in the God who is Love.

A second officer, assigned to accompany the dog handler in their search west of Fletcher Road, had been lagging behind, impeded by the thick, tangled woods, but within less than a minute he struggled out and practically fell over the dead body of his fellow officer and the faithful dog.

Quickly regaining his balance, he got on his phone, "Officer down. I repeat, officer down. Send paramedics immediately. Oh, God, hurry...." He quickly started chest compressions to try to jolt his dead colleague's heart back into beating.

At that very time, Junior was sneaking back into the Little Cannon Creek swamp. Other dogs would undoubtedly try to trail him in his escape, but again, the rubber hip boots would make the scenting difficult. Still, they would now push the search for him even more vigorously....and certainly farther west. He needed a diversion to buy time for his brother and himself. He worked his way downstream in Little Cannon Creek, staying completely hidden from any over-flight, crossing under South Sharon Road through the culvert, until he reached the smaller Silver Creek flowing into it from the south.

He deliberately dropped one of his gloves on the bank right at the junction of the two creeks. Then he got out of the water and seemingly carelessly walked up Silver Creek about a hundred yards or so, leaving his scent on alder bushes and even breaking an occasional branch and leaving the end dangling. Such an obvious trail would immediately capture the attention of both dogs and pursuing officers, and it would be strong evidence that he was working his way south toward the nearby Missaukee County line, maybe trying to get over to State Highway 66 on its way down to Lake City.

In a low, wet spot, he headed back to Silver Creek, and waded carefully and cautiously back downstream to the Little Cannon. Keeping to the water, he chose a particularly dense section of swamp with good standing water and took off north. After about three miles, he was getting close to being back at the cabin in South Swamp.

It was now suppertime, and he was both hyped and fatigued, but he was confident in his escape. Once again Death had stalked the forest, and once again he had left deadly steel in the chest of a state trooper. Nobody could match him in the deep woods. He felt a weird combination of triumphant exhilaration and deep anxiety after this latest murder. One thing he knew: his older brother was going to throw a gasket. He even thought about not telling him, but he knew he had to.

He stopped near the cabin and watched as the daylight was fading around it. If you looked very closely, you could just barely spot the wisp of smoke exiting the chimney pipe. The one window passed no light through its heavy shading except the faintest glow. It also wasn't visible unless you were standing right outside. It was such a great hideaway, but now more than ever, the two brothers had to leave it forever. And leave forever the woman who had been oppressing him for the last three days.

It's all her fault. I wouldn't have gotten involved with her if she hadn't stopped at the truck. She complicated things, and now I've had to kill another stupid trooper as a result. I sure hated to take out the dog. Maybe I should have killed the police pig and taken the dog with me. Nah, that wouldn't have worked. It would have howled like a banshee. And there was probably one or more other officers close behind. Looked like a nice dog, though.

He took a deep breath and braced himself for big brother's tirade. *He's always been such a pain in the ass.*

Family.... He whistled the familiar whippoorwill call to signal his brother to come out, and within a minute Smitty joined him outside in the brush.

CHAPTER EIGHTEEN

"You what? Oh, I cannot believe this. Now they're going to have an army out here on our necks. They'll cut down every tree in the woods to find us. They'll drain every swamp. They'll roll up every little road and two-track to cut off our escape. God Almighty, the hosts of heaven won't be able to stop the blue horde that will blanket this forest. And every sheriff's deputy, every town constable, every school crossing guard will be ready to shoot to kill, you hear me?" He spit as he shook his fist at his baby brother.

Despite the impassioned hyperbole, Junior stood his ground, "Hey, I had no choice. The dog completely surprised me. I mean, what are the chances that it would just stumble across a trail so faint that nothing could follow it? And the cop was right behind it." He proceeded to describe how he had made his escape, especially how he had created a false trail to divert pursuers in the wrong direction.

"Okay, what's done is done. Sending them up Silver Creek toward Missaukee County should buy us that day we need tomorrow...maybe. Well, we don't have much choice, do we? If we take off tonight in a panic, we'll blow it for sure. We have to stick to plan and make triple sure that everything is ready for Wednesday night's departure. I'm going to have to spend more time plotting our route south. They will watch and block every little ant's trail winding through the whole state. We're going to have to be even more vigilant about anyone coming close to here, and even more cautious about finding a way out of here. And don't let on anything to Crystal. If she senses we're panicking, she may just panic herself and do something rash. Let's not have to deal with her until Wednesday at dark."

They went in the cabin for the supper of pancakes and pure Michigan maple syrup that Crystal had fixed for them, along with thick strips of slab bacon that Junior had sliced off earlier with his Bowie knife. They wouldn't entrust Crystal, of course, with any sharp blade.

The silence between the brothers was obvious. Usually they were back and forth with each other, joking, poking, having fun like brothers. Smitty was angry enough to spit, and Junior was even more sullen and silent than usual.

Crystal prudently kept a low profile in the cramped cabin.

Their supper was eaten in almost complete, brooding silence. At one point, Junior asked for the syrup to be passed for his second stack of pancakes, and his big brother had practically shoved the jug at him. Instead of mouthing off in return, Junior practically cowered, and looked down as he poured his syrup.

Maybe this is the time to try to turn the tables, Crystal thought. Up to this point, she had been cowering and submissive herself, being as non-confrontational as possible to avoid any conflict with either of the brothers. But the younger brother seemed vulnerable, whatever the problem was between the two, so she got bold and decided to try a different tactic.

"Can I get you some more bacon?" she asked, knowing that he never refused seconds of just about anything.

"Yah," he replied more softly than he usually spoke.

Crystal got up, went to the woodstove with the bacon plate, used tongs to take several strips of bacon from the fry pan and put them on the plate, and walked back the few feet to the table. Both brothers resumed their sullen, silent eating. When she reached the tabler, she made an effective pretense of stumbling, and dumped the bacon off the plate, some of it falling on the table, but a couple of strips and grease falling into the younger brother's lap.

"Oh, I'm so sorry," she exclaimed. "So clumsy of me. Here, I'll..."

The wound-tight younger brother exploded, "You bitch! I thought you were a waitress, but you're nothing but..."

Instead of shrinking back as usual at his tirade, Crystal slammed the plate down on the table as she had planned and cut him off in mid-sentence.

"I said I'm sorry. It was an accident. And stop calling me 'bitch.' Didn't your momma teach you any better manners? You brought me here against my will, but I've been nice to you and cooked for you and cleaned up after you. And I would have cleaned this up, too, but clean it up yourself. And talk to me with the respect for ladies that your momma would expect." And she pretended to sob and ran over to her corner, where she sat down and continued to cry.

Junior was so taken aback that for a second or two he was speechless. His mind was caught up between images of his momma, grabbing his ear and "teaching him manners," and the sight of his big brother looking at him with still more disgust.

"Now look what you've done, Junior," Smitty barked at him. "Why don't you step outside in the frosty air and cool off. You've created enough trouble for one day."

Junior got up and did as he was told. He liked it better in the forest, anyway. Family, women, cops, they were all just thorns in his flesh. He should have taken off after killing the dog and the handler and not come back at all. He wished he could get his hands on some of that meth and get a nice high going. *Damn them all.* He paced back and forth in the darkness.

Crystal made a pretense of settling down in her crying but kept her head down and smiled to herself. She had taken some control with that incident. How Junior would react she didn't know. He could become more abusive and violent toward her – although he seemed less apt to do that with big brother around – or if it worked as she hoped it would, he could back off some from her. Some space from him would maybe give her room to try her next tactic. She knew she still had to escape, or somehow be rescued, or the time would come before long when they would need to dispose of her. And she had no delusions of them just letting her go down the road somewhere. They would never want to leave a live witness.

Smitty sat at the table by himself for a few moments. He looked at Crystal in the corner, watching her slump over and softly cry on her side, as though she was about to go to sleep.

Was it an accident like she said? She is not a clumsy girl. On the contrary, she usually moves with genuine feminine grace. Did she stage the "accident," and if so, what was she trying to accomplish? Was she just getting back at Junior for abusing her, or was this a play in a more devious plan in her head? However, she did it, the result was to push Junior away from her for the time being.

Bottom line: he knew that he had to continue keeping close watch on the woman. She was up to something. He was sure.

Well, I guess there's no cribbage tonight.

Junior came back in, said nothing, and the two turned in for the night.

CHAPTER NINETEEN

The next morning, Crystal was up, pretending to be hurt and on the verge of tears, but making a big pot of oatmeal for them. The brothers were also more quiet than usual, but at least they were talking to each other, however tensely.

As the darkness of the surrounding swamp started to brighten with the sunrise coming about quarter after 8:00, Smitty spoke the most words since the two of them had gotten up.

"Finish up your bowl of oatmeal, Junior."

"You ain't the boss of me, Smitty."

Smitty glared at his brother, "Oh, but I am, and you know it. So, finish your oatmeal, and we'll get going on gathering up your traps and stakes. We need to get back here and start to put everything in order. Crystal, we're going to have to lock you up in here as usual, but it would be particularly good for you if, while we're gone, you wash and sterilize every cup, glass, plate and bowl in the cupboards. I need to have not a single smudge, not a spot, nothing on any of it. Okay? I need your help and compliance on this, no mistakes."

Crystal wondered just what this "request" was about, why the heightened cleanliness, but she had no trouble catching his meaning. It would not be good for her not to do it. Junior, on the other hand, hadn't said a word to her since he came out of the bedroom, and still didn't as he went out the door with Smitty. They locked her in to do the assigned chores.

She would have to make her move tonight. Her hope was that Smitty would continue to be relatively relaxed with her, and that Junior would continue to keep some distance, virtually ignoring her after their "altercation." She visualized her plan, step by step, and couldn't afford to fail. If they caught her, she knew it would probably be the end for her.

Before the two brothers gathered up the traps and stakes, they went up to higher ground for another close reconnaissance. Junior fervently hoped that the even more intense police search was fruitlessly focused on the Silver Creek area, down to and past the Missaukee County line. At one point they spotted a distant chopper that had to be State Police, but it didn't come close to the cabin location, and before long disappeared over the tree line to the south.

The rest of today, then tomorrow night, Smitty thought to himself. It would seem like an eternity, but they had to stick to plan and hope for the best. At least they would soon be unburdened of Crystal and be moving under the cover of darkness.

"It seems okay for now," he said to Junior. "Let's pick up those traps, and then I'll spend the afternoon in the cabin, going over the county maps, trying to figure the best, backwoods way out of here and heading downstate. You're still the best scout and stalker in the North Woods, Junior.

We need you out here this afternoon, keeping recon for them pushing the search in this direction. You're our only sentinel. But you can't go killing any other dog or cop. Okay?"

"I won't. It was a total fluke. Shouldn't have happened at all. That dog handler was to blame. But I'll set up forward observation posts that can't be approached in any way to catch me off guard. I promise."

When they got back for their Tuesday lunch with all of the traps and stakes, Crystal had all of the cupboard contents out and drying on the table. But she had made more venison sandwiches and put them on paper plates that could be burned that night in the woodstove. She still didn't know what the cleaning project was all about, but if her plan worked, it wouldn't matter. She'd be away from them that night and on her way to safety...she hoped and prayed.

Smitty meticulously inspected each item she had washed and sterilized. Maybe he would do his own wiping of everything, just to be sure, but it looked good. Wednesday's project before their departure would be to wipe down every bit of the interior of the cabin, the cache, and even the outhouse. That was assuming the frantic search for Junior, the unknown murderer of two state police officers, wasn't successful before then. Smitty had the on-edge feeling that whatever happened, however this all played out, it would be a "skin of the teeth" ending. Either the two brothers would pull the narrow escape of all time, or the intensely angry authorities would just barely catch them...alive or dead. Too bad Crystal wouldn't be alive for that dramatic ending. She was a nice girl, however devious she turned out to be.

Smitty spent almost three hours going over his maps, marking the most obscure unpaved roads and two-tracks, figuring a serpentine course for their working their way south. The cops couldn't block every little route, and if they stuck to his marks, and scouted ahead at each step, he thought they could make it out of Michigan and into Ohio. It was their only hope of escape.

Junior, meanwhile, spent his time acting as their scout and sentinel. True to his word, whether on post or moving silently through the forest and swamps, he was invisible and soundless. At one point he noted movement downstream on Little Cannon Creek, below the junction with Silver Creek. They were still searching down in that area, but it was only a matter of time before they would move outward even farther and draw closer to the cabin. He hoped that it would take them the rest of today, until dark, and all of Wednesday before getting into South Swamp. But they were most certainly coming, and they were coming with wrath and vengeance in their hearts. Smitty and he just needed to be gone before they arrived.

He got back to the cabin shortly before dark descended upon the swamp. Before Junior went in, he checked the top of the chimney pipe. It looked good, very little smoke coming out, and very little breeze to carry the odor. As he entered, Smitty had finished his mapping project. Crystal was stirring a pot of venison chili on the wood stove.

He had three bowls of the warming chili and crackers. They were disposable paper bowls, and when the three had finished their meal, the bowls and plastic spoons went into the fire. Since everyone had settled down from the previous evening, the cribbage board came out again. Crystal played two games with the brothers, then yawned, expressed her fatigue, and withdrew to her corner. Junior kept avoiding conversation with her and again ignored her as much as possible. But on the bright side for Crystal, he didn't call her "bitch" or act particularly abusive toward her during the entire meal and cards after.

Smitty and Junior played a third game, but it was considerably more subdued than they usually played, with little bluster or celebrating when Junior managed to win. Smitty frankly felt tense and on edge with the developments of the last two days, and Junior was tired after yet another day of reconnaissance out in the forest and swamps, so the two retired to the bedroom a bit earlier than usual.

Without appearing to do so, Crystal watched the two like a proverbial hawk. For three nights now she had secretly observed their bedtime habits, since they routinely kept the bedroom door open for heat from the stove until they were ready to slip under their blankets. Smitty would remove his shirt and pants, fold them rather neatly, and place them on a small chest at the foot of his cot. He liked to go to sleep on his left side, and since he had taken the unused cot on the right when he arrived, he would be facing the wall as he fell asleep.

But it was the younger brother that most interested Crystal. He was much less tidy, and when he took off his shirt and pants, he tended to toss them on the floor at the foot of his cot on the left side. After Smitty rolled over to face the wall, Junior would routinely get up and close the bedroom door. She didn't know what his preferred position was when going to sleep, but she had heard him snoring quite loudly each night shortly after turning in and guessed that he probably went to sleep on his back.

She waited a good long while, listening to the usual snoring behind the bedroom door. Finally, she got up in her bare feet and tiptoed over to listen at the door for a while more. No change that she could detect, and no noise on the other side of the door except Junior's snoring. Now would come the hard part. She would carefully open the door – she had thought ahead to smear a small amount of the bacon grease on the top and bottom hinges to try to eliminate any squeaking – and she would sneak over to Junior's shirt and pants crumpled on the floor.

She knew that he always kept the inside cabin lock keys in his right-hand pants pocket. She would have to slip them out without any jangling, ease the pants back down to the floor noiselessly, tiptoe back through the door, and silently close it again. Then, she could very carefully and quietly unlock the interior lock on the cabin door, step out unheard into the night, and sneak up the overgrown path. She would have to watch out for the noisy "alarm system" Junior was so proud of, but if she moved slowly and with small steps, she should be able to detect it before it made a clatter.

Even in the dark, once she got to where the car was camouflaged among the aspen trees, she could feel her way along the barely visible two-track lane that approached the vicinity of the cabin. She would just keep picking her way along all through the night. She hoped she would reach a better gravel road before sunup and before the brothers woke up to find her gone. She needed to keep her ears open to any sounds to her rear. If she heard any possible pursuit on their part, she would need to get off the two-track and try to find somewhere to hide, hoping that they would pass by.

She took a deep breath and slowly opened the bedroom door. No squeaking, and no other noise, a good start. She went step by step slowly over to Junior's heaped up clothes and started to feel for his right pants pocket. She closed her hand around the key chain, but as she withdrew the keys, her bracelet caught on the pocket slit, startled her, and she dropped the key chain back into his pants pocket, onto the floor.

The sound was slight, but Junior was right about himself. He was a light sleeper – almost "one eye open" – and his head jerked upward from his position on his back.

Crystal instantly reacted by whispering, "Oh, I'm so sorry to bother you sir, but I came in to get you because I *really* have to use the outhouse. I wouldn't ask, but any second now

I'll pee my pants. I'm really sorry."

Half asleep, Junior was greatly annoyed, but after all that had happened, he feared waking his big brother. "Get back outta here. Wait for me out there." He muttered and grumbled under his breath as Crystal snuck back to the main room. *Damn she's nothing but trouble. If I'd been more awake, I should have told her to use a coffee can.* Nonetheless, he pulled on his pants, slipped a sweatshirt over his head, and put his boots on without socks. His big brother continued to snore lightly.

Waiting for Junior to emerge from the bedroom, Crystal was silently frantic about her failed effort. She didn't have a Plan B. Her mind raced. *Should I wait until he goes outside with me, grab a piece of that firewood stacked outside and knock him senseless? Should I just take off running?*

As Junior shoved her out the cabin door toward the outhouse, she forced her runaway emotions to calm down. With him behind her, there was no chance of grabbing that hunk of firewood. If she ran, he'd catch her in no time and there'd be hell to pay. She had no choice but to bide her time for the rest of the night, try as hard as she could to mollify his temper, and try to figure out some other way to escape.

But she had an overwhelming feeling that whatever effort she made, it had to be tomorrow. She had heard them talking about Wednesday. The extra cleaning efforts were a tip-off, and she had observed both of them slipping things into backpacks and duffles. They were preparing to leave, and she couldn't see a good reason that they would want to take her with them. Even more than before, Crystal felt like something to be discarded.

Coming back out of the outhouse, she made herself grovel as much as possible.

"Oh, thank you. I couldn't have held it a minute more. I'm so-o sorry to have wakened you. It won't happen again."

"Damn straight it won't. Now get back in the cabin." There was just a hint in his tone that he knew she'd never be able to disturb his sleep, or anything about him, ever again. Crystal was at the peak of her fear and her desperation to do *something* to survive.

CHAPTER TWENTY

Danny and Andrea were up early that Wednesday morning. They packed up their picnic items in an antique picnic basket Andrea inherited from her grandmother. Danny was dressed in a red and black, checkered, flannel shirt and jeans and hiking boots for their Wednesday afternoon outing with Tiny and Angela. Andrea had to go into the post for the morning but would be off for the afternoon as she had scheduled with the desk sergeant.

"You're sure it's okay for you to take this afternoon off?" Danny checked with her one more time.

"They said it would be okay. My TNT group met Monday morning, as you know. We went over all the files and past cases I had pulled out on Sunday. We assigned officers to contact their confidential informants – 'CI's' – for any chatter about any new drug lab someone may have set up. They put that word out and offered bigger than usual 'bonuses' for new information Monday afternoon. Those contacts were followed up on Tuesday, as well as surveillance on past and present drug houses, garages, sheds, wherever a meth lab had been or might be now. They're keeping hidden surveillance this morning, and we could have sprung our raids today, but as I said before, Thursday morning the DEA and FBI agents are due to arrive and beef up our forces, so everything is on hold for today."

"We can always hope that the search teams and dogs finally catch up with this guy in the forest today. And now he's murdered another trooper?" Danny shook his head in dismay.

"Yes. It's just horrible," Andrea looked almost ready to shed a tear. "A crossbow arrow took out his tracking dog first, and then another fired in quick succession killed the handler."

"And they couldn't run him down? He must be good...I'm sorry, you know what I mean," Danny winced apologetically.

"As before with Trooper Baldwin, he apparently sticks to streams, wet swamps, places where the dogs can't scent him or pick up his trail. They've never had such an elusive perpetrator before. He has to be a highly experienced woodsman, so part of the deeper investigation is checking with sporting goods stores, rod and gun clubs, outdoorsman groups or associations – looking for a tip or lead on that rare individual who's known for exceptional skills in the wild."

"But you think running down the meth lab may be the key to finding him."

"I do," Andrea nodded firmly. "Somebody in the Grand Traverse area cooked that meth. He picked it up, undoubtedly for distribution downstate somewhere, so whoever put it into his hands to deliver knows who he is. They still haven't been able to find Wes Smith, so since it was his rusty old truck that got stuck near the North Branch of the Manistee, he's probably our number one suspect for now."

"You don't sound entirely convinced, though," Danny observed.

"No. As we've known for years, Wes is trouble waiting to happen. But as I've said before, he's never been particularly violent in his scrapes with the law, or when I've pulled him over for speeding and DUI. Nothing more than making excuses and trying to dodge being written up. Murdering not just one, but now two, state police troopers is way out of his league. Although you never know for sure. Maybe something snapped or drastically changed deep down inside him, and he's become capable of much worse than he was before."

"Well, with all of this going on, I hope our time this afternoon will be a welcome break from the stress, tension and grief. I'm so sorry for you," Danny said with all the sincerity he was capable of, "and all of your fellow officers. I keep your state police family in my prayers morning, afternoon and night."

"I know you do, honey. I do, too...and dozens of people at church, the whole prayer chain, and others. But I need to get in there. I have my hiking clothes and boots in the car, so I can change at the post when I check out," she brightened and smiled so beautifully it fanned his constant love for her.

"And Tiny and Angela will meet us in your parking lot there?"

"Yes," she affirmed. "It'll be no trouble for them to leave their Lincoln in a corner of the lot while we're out for the afternoon, and we'll all go in your Grand Cherokee, of course."

"And then it's off to check out Uncle Jake's old, log cabin and what remains of this gorgeous fall color," Danny smiled.

As Andrea went out the door in her uniform, she called back, "And don't forget to fill the thermoses just before you come to meet me."

"You got it...hot coffee and hot cider with cinnamon sticks. And those great Northern Spy apples we got at the farmer's market," he called after her as she got in her Santa Fe and drove off to the post on the other side of Traverse City. This day was going to be so much fun.

CHAPTER TWENTY-ONE

About 45 minutes after leaving the State Police Post on 14th Street in Traverse City, close to 1:00 P.M., Danny, Andrea, Tiny and Angela were headed south on State Highway 66 in the town of Kalkaska. They passed the city fountain with the big, leaping statue of a brightly colored brook trout, and Tiny pointed, "Now that's really a big one." The four laughed and felt good about being so close to their destination. At West Sharon Road, Danny turned east toward the Big Manistee River. After crossing the Manistee, the next turn was south on an unpaved, gravel road deeper into the forest.

As the gravel road seemed to grow rougher, Andrea looked for a branched two-track lane that came out to the gravel road from the south. She told Danny when to turn, and they bumped up and down on the two-track as it wound into the deep woods, made a large curve, and then angled toward a big cedar swamp. A couple of two-track branches took off at different spots, each appearing almost too narrow for a vehicle to navigate, but Andrea had him stick to what passed for the primary lane. Tiny was watching from the back seat as they worked a couple of miles or so into this thick part of the forest.

"You know," he whispered to Angela, "we probably need to keep close to these two, or we may never find our way out of here."

"I know," she whispered back. "I felt lost as soon as we left the gravel road."

Before reaching the low, wet swampy ground, they twisted their way on the two-track to a very small opening surrounding by thick, maturing aspens that still clung to many of their golden, browning, twisting leaves.

"Here's the parking spot for Uncle Jake's cabin," Andrea announced. "We have to hike a couple of hundred yards into the swamp from here."

"Oh, it's just beautiful," Angela exclaimed, "It seems so wild and unspoiled here. And these aspen with the tall pines behind them, just gorgeous...but what's that over there?"

"I don't know," Andrea looked, "but it looks like camouflage netting pulled over a car."

"Who would do that way back in here?" Danny wondered. "Wouldn't be anyone you know, would it?"

"I certainly don't think anyone in my family would be here," Andrea replied, puzzled. "Let's get out and take a closer look."

All four of them got out of the Jeep and walked over to the hidden car. They tried looking through the netting and peering into the windows, but really couldn't make out much inside the car. There were boot tracks outside the driver's side, however, and one of them caught Andrea's eye and put her on high alert.

"Look, Danny, this one print in the soft sand has that small, ragged notch in the sole. It's the same track that was left on the berm of Highway 72 at the spot where Trooper Baldwin was murdered."

"You're sure, hon?"

"Definitely. They sent us all photos of the casts that were made. This is the same boot track. Do you still have your Ruger .22 pistol locked in the bottom of the console of the Jeep?"

"Ah, sure," Danny affirmed. "To be honest, I never stopped carrying it there after Ken Romano was trying to ambush me."

"Good," Andrea stated with a stern look. "Get it out for me. We're going to check this out and see if someone's been using Uncle Jake's cabin. But we're only going to scout the place from a distance. If we see evidence that someone's broken in there and is there now, we back off and I'll call dispatch. It shouldn't take too long for search vehicles and squads of troopers to get over here from the primary search area. We could probably have a chopper here in fifteen minutes."

Danny went back to the Grand Cherokee, unlocked the console, and got out the holstered Ruger pistol. He handed it to Andrea, who ran her belt through the slots of the holster, but kept the handgun in her right hand, ready for any unwelcome surprise.

"Tiny, maybe Angela and you should stay here in the Jeep. I don't want to expose you to any danger."

"Uh-uh," Tiny protested. "We're sticking with you two."

Angela was alarmed and felt rather frightened, but she agreed, "You're not going to leave me here, lost in this forest primeval. I go where you go."

"Okay, but Danny," Andrea ordered, "stay right behind me on the path, and Tiny and Angela, single file behind him. And everybody move slowly and as quietly as possible. We don't want to announce our presence in case someone really is at the cabin. Let's move."

Andrea pushed into the thick brush as Danny followed, with Tiny and Angela watching them go and looking quizzically at each other. What path? But several yards into the woods ahead of them, a slight, deer trail-like path started to show up on the forest floor. It gradually wound its way through the trees, sloping ever so slightly down into the swamp.

The dark, thick, cedar and hemlock trees began to be visible ahead through the hardwoods and pines, and Danny knew that they were reaching the edge of the swamp and its entangled creek. Andrea put her left hand up in a stop signal, and then turned her palm down to indicate that they should all get down low. Danny, Tiny, and Angela crept quietly up to her side.

The four looked down from their high ground into the flood plain of the cedar swamp creek. The faint path started to slope down a bit more steeply ahead and to the right...where a dark shape seemed to form through the thick foliage.

"There," Andrea whispered, "see the cabin roof? It's tucked hard against this slope from the dry, high ground down to the swampy area."

"Wow," Danny exclaimed softly, "unless you knew what to look for, you wouldn't even know it was here."

The four of them stayed hunkered down for several minutes, not moving, and not talking, just watching for any sign of activity or occupancy at the cabin. Finally, Tiny whispered, "Look, is that just a small wisp of smoke coming out of the chimney pipe?"

"Yeah," Angela chimed in, "I thought I smelled just a hint of wood smoke in the air, but I wasn't sure."

"Somebody's definitely been using it," Andrea concluded. "I haven't been here for probably five years or more, and I know nobody else in my family has, either. In fact, I'm the only one who has keys now. Follow me back up the trail, and when we get back to the Jeep, I'm calling dispatch. That boot track is enough evidence to call in the force."

She carefully backed up, quietly turned in the direction in which they had come, and Danny stayed right behind her. Angela tiptoed behind him, and Tiny was about to bring up the rear when a desperate figure suddenly crashed up the path from the cabin, screaming.

CHAPTER TWENTY-TWO

Wednesday morning the two brothers had spent most of their time washing and wiping down every surface in the cabin. They pressed Crystal into joining them, at the same time keeping a close watch on her work to make sure that she wasn't deliberately leaving any evidence for the authorities to find. All three wore gloves.

The fire in the wood stove was allowed to burn down and almost out after their final breakfast at the cabin. Smitty also went out to the cache to clear it of any trace evidence of their presence. The brothers decided that Junior would watch over Crystal as they had her scrub down the interior of the outhouse.

Crystal would have felt nauseous and disgusted at having to clean the smelly outhouse thoroughly, but her mind was sharply focused on her captivity and some, any, way to escape. She knew what was happening – the brothers would be gone by nightfall, and she was dead certain they wouldn't be taking her with them.

All they needed to take with them had been removed from the cabin and stacked up outside to be toted up the little path. Everything to be left behind in the cabin had been washed and sterilized. All prints had been washed or wiped away. They had required Crystal to make cold venison sandwiches for a late lunch, which they ate in the small clearing in which the cabin sat, so as not to contaminate the sanitized interior. Junior had thought to have each of them put gunny sack shoe covers over their shoes before making any final steps into the cabin.

It was approaching 2:00, and sundown wouldn't be for another four hours and a bit, but just about all of their preparations had been made. Junior had taken brief breaks that morning to do close-in reconnaissance around the cabin, and despite hearing helicopter noise to the south, no one had been spotted drawing closer to their location. About mid-morning he also dismantled his crude but effective alarm system along the faint little path.

Crystal had been working and washing non-stop and was already exhausted as she munched on her sandwich. Water drawn from the clean creek provided their beverages, since the brothers had packed up the remaining bottles of beer and the coffee pot had been scrubbed clean. They were sitting on cut pieces of log, and the combination of the uncomfortable seats and the hard cleaning activity of the day made Crystal's back feel strained and cramped. She arched her back and stretched to try to loosen her muscles.

Junior had finished his sandwich, got up, and headed for the outhouse. "I gotta take a dump. Back in a few."

Smitty cautioned him to be sure to sit on magazine pages, then put a match to them when he got up and brush the ashes into the hole. "We don't need your ass leaving any DNA or ass-prints on that seat."

As Junior walked over and opened the outhouse door,

Smitty continued to watch Crystal trying to stretch and loosen her back. Her flannel shirt was almost thoroughly soaked from her washing for hours, and her ample breasts did their own stretching of the shirt front. The brothers had agreed to wait until it was getting dark to force themselves upon her, have their way with her, and, well, dispose of her in the swamp. *But damn, she's getting me aroused now.*

Smitty decided it wouldn't hurt to get a piece of Crystal now...and then maybe again before they left. He moved over to the section of log on her left, smiled leeringly, and tried to whisper in her ear, "You're turning me on, woman."

Crystal had been thinking and thinking all morning of how and when she might make her desperate attempt to get away from them, kept rejecting possible moments to make a break for it, and felt increasing anxious about the fact that they were always scrutinizing her activity. Her eyes had been almost closed when she was trying to stretch, so Smitty's move to draw closer to her caught her by surprise.

When he put his hand palm down on the piece of log she was sitting on and leaned close to whisper in her left ear, she panicked, almost reflexively reached deep into her right jeans pocket and grabbed the fork that she had kept hidden. In a lightning-quick blow, she swung the fork over and down and buried its tines in the back of Smitty's hand. She was almost as surprised as he was, not having planned the desperate strike, but he was much more painfully stunned.

"Goddamn!" he hollered "Shit, you little..." And words broke up into sputters and moans as he grabbed his right hand with his left, the fork sticking out and blood spraying in all directions.

Crystal, meanwhile, took off like a sprinter up the path toward the place where they had hidden Smitty's car. Junior heard the commotion, swung open the outhouse door, and came stumbling out, trying to pull up his pants and zip up in the same motion. The normally stealthy backwoodsman practically fell trying to run over to where his older brother was gripping his bleeding hand, the fork still stuck there.

"Go get her," Smitty hollered as Junior ran up to him. "She attacked me with a goddamned fork." He tried to think of what to wrap around his bleeding hand once they pulled the fork out. Junior grabbed the handle of his Bowie knife, pulled it out of the sheath on his belt, and took off after Crystal, who had already disappeared in the thick brush on both sides of the path.

I knew I should have gotten rid of the bitch. I knew it. Well, woman, your time has run out. We were almost done with you, anyhow.

He was chasing a dead woman. She had no woods craft. No matter where she tried to run in the dense forest, he'd catch her and kill her quicker than he did those cops. She was just making it easier for him, running up the path, screaming like she was.

CHAPTER TWENTY-THREE

Panicked and screaming involuntarily, Crystal ran almost blindly...right into the massive form of the biggest, blackest man she had ever stood next to. The giant Tiny reached out, trying to catch her as she literally smacked into him, and he tried to hush her.

"There, there, you're okay. You're safe. Who you running from? What's going on, girl?"

But not hearing nor comprehending and terrified at what seemed a new threat, Crystal spun around and irrationally ran back down the path...right into the grasp of the pursuing Junior, who gripped her with his left hand and held the knife to her throat with his right.

Andrea took several steady steps forward down the path and was soon greeted with the sight of the enraged Junior, big knife drawn at Crystal's throat. It was completely unlike Junior to have anyone sneak up on him and surprise him, and his eyes widened at the sight of Andrea moving toward him in the brush, pistol drawn. Others were behind her. He couldn't see through the foliage just how many. There was no time to ponder who they were or how they had gotten so close without him knowing.

"Police! Stop right there, hands over your head," Andrea commanded with all the authority she possessed. "Drop the knife. Let go of the woman! Let me see your hand! Now!"

Junior would do no such thing, of course, and he pushed Crystal back down the path to the cabin as fast as he could get her to go.

Smitty was still clutching his bleeding hand, although he had gone back into the cabin and wrapped an old dish towel around it. "Who is it? The police find us?"

"Yah, 'fraid so. Come on, we gotta get outta here."

Smitty grabbed his baby brother with his good, left hand. "You go. I'll stay here and stall them. I haven't killed anyone, and they can't trace the meth to me, either. In fact, I'll claim you held me captive, too. By the time they figure out who's telling the truth – the girl or me – you can be far away in the swamp."

"I can't leave you, bro'" Junior protested. "You're my family."

"Yah, and that's why you have to do it. So long as you're free, it's like our family is free and kings of the forest. I'll be okay, now get outta here."

"Okay, but I'm taking the bitch as a hostage."

There was no time to argue further. Andrea, Danny and Tiny were moving cautiously down the path with Angela close behind. Spotting the figures of the brothers through the brush as they stood, arguing in the little cabin clearing, Andrea repeated her commands to stop where they were, put their hands up over their heads where she could see them, and kneel down in the dirt.

Smitty complied, figuring that it would put her off-guard a bit, but Junior, keeping a firm grip on Crystal, scuffled over to their pile of stuff to be taken up and loaded in the car. He grabbed his dependable crossbow with several arrows secured in a holder attached to the bow. He hustled her down to the creek and plunged into the wet cedar swamp, quickly disappearing from view.

With Andrea in the lead, Ruger leveled and aimed with both hands, the four best friends came into the small opening in front of the cabin and circled around the older brother.

"Well as I live and breathe," Andrea said, looking down at their prisoner, "if it isn't Wes Smith. You're in a lot more trouble than driving a few miles over the limit and having a few too many beers. Here, Danny, put this zip-tie around his wrists. Now, tell me about the man and the woman you've had with you."

CHAPTER TWENTY-FOUR

J unior pulled Crystal, stumbling and virtually falling, downstream through the creek and its surrounding cedar swamp. It was like the middle of the night early Saturday morning all over again, hauling this bothersome woman behind him, but this time it wouldn't be for so long. She kept screaming and crying, so as soon as they were well out of sight, he stopped for a few seconds, fished a partial roll of duct tape out of a deep pocket in his camo overalls, and slapped it over her mouth.

Damn it's hard to think with her carrying on like that. That'll make things more quiet for now. And they resumed splashing downstream.

The creek was winding, gurgling by and under cedar and hemlock logs and leaning-over trees, irresistibly in the general direction of the Big Manistee. He knew full well that his area of relative safety was shrinking drastically by now. He couldn't head anywhere south or east – that area was gripped by the dragnet tightening around him. North was out of the question, it squeezed him between the Manistee River and the little crossroads of Sharon. He couldn't afford to try to drift down the river – he would be completely exposed on the big water, and he knew from the beginning that it was one of the first possible avenues of escape the pigs would watch.

But before anything else, he had to worry about the close pursuit of what police were now at the cabin, which is really why he had grabbed Crystal and forced her to go with him again. He knew well enough that having her as a hostage wouldn't give him any advantage in trying to get away. They would go to great lengths to try to rescue her, but at the same time, there was no way they would let him release her and simply escape. But release her he would, very soon now.

He had wrestled her maybe three hundred yards or so downstream with him, but surprised her by stopping and even removing the tape from her mouth. He held the big knife up before her terrified eyes as a deadly threat, keeping her breathless and quiet as she could be while gasping and struggling for air.

By God's truth, I would have no trouble gutting her right here and now, but I have a more important purpose for the bitch...and at last I can be rid of her and the trouble she's been determined to cause me from the beginning.

Not even seeing what he was doing, Crystal shrieked in excruciating pain as Junior reached down and slashed across the back of her boot and her left Achilles heel. He didn't cut all the way through the vital tendon, but it was more than enough to cripple her and cause her to collapse in the shallow creek water, blood spurting.

While she moaned painfully, he turned to go on farther downstream.

"Goodbye, Crystal, that's what you get for causing me so much grief. Be thankful you're still alive. And maybe some man won't mind your limp." He seemed to take perverse pleasure in his brutal action and his cruel comment that first and only time he referred to her by name. And then he was gone.

It was a calculated move, of course. Her screams and moans would lead the cops right to her. At least two of them, maybe even more, would be required to transport the crippled woman out of the creek and its jungle-like swamp...which was why, of course, he had waited to do what he did. It would buy him time, and he desperately needed time and space from his pursuers.

When Junior had grabbed Crystal and hauled her after him into the swampy creek, Andrea held up from firing as they disappeared for fear of hitting the woman.

"Don't keep me waiting, Wes," she demanded. "Who are they?"

Wes didn't see any advantage in playing dumb at that point. "It's my younger brother, Junior, and the woman he kidnapped early Saturday morning. But it's no use you going after him. If he doesn't want to be found in the forest, you won't find him. He's like a ghost, a will-o-the-wisp. The tracking dogs can't catch up with him. No one can."

Softly but confidently, Angela spoke up: "I can."

Wes "Smitty" Smith looked in her direction, "I recognize you. You're that clerk from the gift store in Suttons Bay. A townie like you, catch Junior in the swamp? Not in a damn sight," he snorted derisively.

Angela ignored him and spoke earnestly to Andrea, Danny, and Tiny. "No, really, I can track him. You remember," she looked up at Tiny, "my grandmother on my mother's side was pure Apache. When I was a kid growing up in South Central Los Angeles, my mom used to send me to Grandma and Grandpa's ranch in Arizona for the summer when school was out. Every day my grandmother would take me out to the far pastures, the woods, the mountain streams, the rocky washes, the buttes, and teach me how to track. Eventually I would be rewarded by being taken into town for ice cream if I could follow a single trail across bare rock and through swift water. I can track him."

Andrea would have been paralyzed by the wonder of what Angela was telling them, but there was no time simply to be amazed. Quick action was needed.

"Okay, Tiny, your bum knees won't hold up in that cold water and tangled swamp, anyway, so you sit on Wes and don't let him so much as wiggle."

Wes looked up at the menacing bulk of Tiny and his eyes widened. "Oh, no, not you again. You're the guy who squashed me like a bug against my own truck door." Tiny just nodded and grinned ominously.

"Here," Andrea gave Tiny her cell phone. My dispatch is on speed dial. Call the desk. Let them know to GPS us here at the cabin and to send troopers and dogs and the chopper ASAP. Angela will lead me in going after Junior and the woman. We have to rescue her before he does anything bad to her. If he decides that she's slowing him down, he may slit her throat to shed himself of her."

"Well, I'm going, too," Danny insisted. "We're in this together 'til the very end."

"Here's my cell," Tiny said, exchanging his for Andrea's. "Call me as soon as you have an update. Hopefully as soon as you've caught him and rescued her."

Crystal's pained scream rang through the swamp from downstream. "Come on," Andrea ordered, "we don't have time to argue. Let's get this bastard."

With Angela leading the way, the three entered the swampy water and headed with urgency in the direction that Junior had taken. Before long, the downstream current split into two primary channels, one gurgling under low-hanging hemlocks and cedars to the left, the other stream disappearing under a log jam to the right.

Angela stopped momentarily, bent over, and scrutinized both directions.

"Come on," she pointed to the right, "he took her this way."

Danny couldn't help himself. Ever the inquisitive thinker, he asked, "But how do you know?"

"See this log lodged against the roots of this cedar? There's a fresh scrape of the moss on it...and, look, the log behind it is dry on top, but has fresh drops of water from where they stepped over it."

The three continued, but neither Danny nor Andrea asked any more questions. It seemed more than clear that Angela really did know what she was doing when it came to tracking. Before long, they could hear moans and crying up ahead, growing louder as they proceeded downstream. They fought their way under low-hanging cedar branches and spotted Crystal, lying just out of the water on the muddy bank, partially under a hemlock branch that swept down almost to ground level. She continuously moaned and cried, and as they drew close to her, they could see her left ankle and foot was covered in blood.

"Quickly," Andrea ordered Danny and Angela, "give me handkerchiefs, a bandana, strips of your shirts, anything we can use to wrap around her wound and slow the blood loss."

Danny put his arm under Crystal and lifted her to a sitting position.

"He cut me," she moaned and shivered from the combination of the cold afternoon and the blood loss. "Why did he have to cut me? I wasn't fighting him." And she sobbed uncontrollably.

They knew why he had waited until then to injure her so severely. He had to slow his pursuers. He had more of a lead on them now.

"You're going to be okay now," Andrea assured her. "He won't be able to hurt you anymore. You're safe with us, and we're going to get you medical help. Just hang on."

"You're really brave," Danny encouraged Crystal. "You've survived and you're going to be okay."

Their words pushed through her pain and fear, started to sink in, and she found the strength to nod in agreement and gratitude. "Thank you, oh, thank you for rescuing me." As Danny continued to support her, he looked up at Andrea and Angela.

"My love," he spoke to Andrea, "you're going to have to take care of...what's your name, ma'am? Crystal...okay, you need to stay with Crystal, hon, and coordinate with the search team that will arrive at any moment now. Angela seems to be the only one capable of tracking the bastard in this beastly swamp, and I better go with her to back her up. You better give me the Ruger. We can't let this double murderer fade away again."

Andrea looked at him, at Angela, and then at Crystal, her blood loss slowed, but drenching the cloths wrapped around her ankle. "Oh, no, I don't like that option at all. Maybe all three of us should concentrate on getting Crystal to a more comfortable place and wait for the manpower and firepower to arrive."

"But Andrea," Angela protested, "you heard from that Wes Smith how his brother is such a super woodsman. And if the tracking dogs haven't been able to trail him and corner him in these swamps, well, frankly I may be the only one who can do it."

"Yeah," Danny joined her argument. "We can't take the chance that he'll escape again. And someone has to stay and help Crystal and the searchers."

Andrea handed over the Ruger pistol with great

reluctance and was most definitely not happy with the situation. But their arguments were compelling, and the more they dawdled, the farther away Junior Smith would get. She turned to give her full attention to Crystal and her horrible wound, and called Tiny on the cell phone to give him that update he had asked for.

"Have troopers showed up at the cabin yet?" she asked anxiously.

"No, not yet," Tiny replied, "but I think they will soon. I think I hear vehicles approaching up on the high ground."

"Well, we have the woman," Andrea reported, "but she's badly cut and needs medical attention ASAP. Send officers and paramedics downstream as soon as you can, and I'll make more than enough racket that they'll be able to find us."

She was going to report as well on Danny and Angela continuing the pursuit of the murderer, but just then Crystal shouted out painfully as she tried to move her left leg and foot, and Andrea turned to help her and signed off from Tiny for the time being.

CHAPTER TWENTY-FIVE

Junior moved more easily and less noisily without the uncooperative burden of the bitch. He slipped almost silently downstream, making very little splashing, and carefully parted intertwining branches that hung over the creek. When the surrounding swamp widened, he veered at an angle away from the creek proper, followed a smaller branch of flowing water, and came alongside a low, thickly wooded hill rising up from the low, wet ground around it.

The good-sized hillock was well known to him. It was a favorite place for deer to bed, to stay dry and hidden in the surrounding swamp, and to be alert for any predators – whether animal or human – that might approach, splashing in the wet swamp all around. Consequently, it was also a favorite hunting spot for bobcats, coyotes, foxes, and an occasional bear, since not only deer, but also snowshoe hares, grouse, plentiful mice and porcupines, and other prey would be found using the low but dry ground it provided.

He stepped as lightly as he could manage on the dry

ground, expertly sure to distribute his weight evenly with each step, so that his boots would disturb very little vegetation and make very little mark on any soil upon which he trod. The Native Americans of long ago would sneak like that on their forest trails, and he was confident that he could do it as well, or better even.

Junior skirted the west edge of the low-lying hillock, made a circle clockwise toward the north end, and came back in a hook toward the east edge, coming to a stop in a dense thicket growing on the highest point of the dry ground. There were three active deer beds in the thicket, but the deer were out in feeding grounds that early evening, so they were unused when he settled in. It was a perfect vantage point to watch his back trail. It was unlikely to the extreme that anyone could have followed him through all the creek tangle and the swampiness to reach this hideaway, but good woods craft enabled him to make sure. For about an hour he watched as the sun slid down toward the horizon. Sure enough, no pursuit, he congratulated himself. The stupid cops were probably all atwitter about the dumb bitch and the injury she had brought upon herself.

He was almost lulled into drowsiness when some silent movement caught his eye down where he had gone through to the south and west.

What is that? Probably a deer. No, too big...and there's another form with it. Damn, how did they follow me here? I left no trail. He puzzled this unexpected development while he got ready to move out.

"Look," Angela whispered to Danny. "See where his boot dislodged that small stone and left some crumbled dirt where the stone had been?"

Danny had to look really low to the ground and squint to see what she was talking about, but sure enough, there was a small stone dislodged and turned over, leaving a depressed spot in the soil where the stone had laid previously. How could anyone discern such a faint trail? Angela had always impressed him for other reasons, but he was increasingly in awe of this ability she kept displaying.

"And see where he stepped in that shallow puddle, and then left just a little moisture on the flat rock beyond the puddle. Now if we had been here another 30 minutes to an hour later, that small amount of moistness would probably have evaporated to the point of being invisible or gone completely. That's why it's so important to keep after him, or else the trail becomes harder to pick out."

Danny shook his head in amazement at her perceptiveness and tracking knowledge. He wasn't the only one being amazed. Junior slipped silently out of his sentinel thicket and stepped gingerly down to the wet, swampy ground to the north and east of the hillock. He shook his head that he was going to have to find an even more secure hiding place.

Maybe I'll even need more of a discouragement to my pursuers, he thought. They always say that the best defense is a good offense, he smiled deviously to himself. He knew just the place to go.

Angela led Danny to the top of the small hill and readily found the thicket, its deer beds, and the exact spot where Junior had set himself down to watch his back trail.

"Well, it doesn't surprise me that he knows we're after him," she whispered to Danny. "Here's where he hunkered down to watch his back trail for any pursuers."

"Crap," Danny spit out softly. "I was hoping we could catch up to him before he really knew we were so close."

"Not likely," Angela replied. "This guy is as good as ol' Wes boasted. His trail is almost indiscernible, and he's as cautious as a mature, wounded buck watching for hunters tracking it."

Danny looked downcast and discouraged, but said nothing. Angela spoke softly again, "But hey, this is actually good."

"How so?" he puzzled.

"Well, now that he knows we can track him even in these difficult conditions, and that we were catching up to him, he may get unsettled enough to start making some mistakes. You know, inadvertently leave more 'sign' than he would if he could move more slowly and precisely."

"And no 'prey' likes to know that its predator is after it and closing in," Danny responded more brightly. But then he furrowed his brow again, "But it will be getting dark before long. Won't we lose his trail then and he'll give us the slip?"

Angela laughed quietly, "Well, I can track by flashlight and sometimes even by moonlight. But I have to admit it's even harder than what we're doing now. But when night falls, he'll slow down, too, and probably find a place to rest and get some shut-eye like a deer when it beds down. If we don't catch up to him soon, we'll mark the place on his trail where we left off. And remember, we have Crystal now, and we can take as much time as we need to run this 'fox' to ground. We'll have him tomorrow when we have a lot more pursuers to join in the hunt. Or the next day at the latest. He's going to run out of places to run to and hide, you know."

Yeah, Danny thought to himself, *but don't they always say that a cornered wild beast is the most dangerous?* There was light yet, though, so Angela and he followed Junior's scant trail out of the thicket and into the wetland.

CHAPTER TWENTY-SIX

Junior soon reached a small, unnamed feeder creek in the swamp. It soon opened up to a marshy, mucky area with an old beaver lodge in the middle. In the few years that he had visited the spot, there was usually a pair of beavers that raised their family there. The water was shallow around the lodge, and the feeder creek kept it from drying up in the hot summer.

If his pursuers were as good as they seemed to be and were still on his trail, they would slog after him, reach the edge where the tangled cedars gave way to the little patch of marsh grass, and be forced to step out into the open at least briefly, facing the beaver lodge. Junior crept to the far side of the lodge, nestled himself among the dry branches on top of the lodge, and was confident that his camo overalls and hat would keep him from being seen when they came out to the opening. He armed his deadly crossbow with an arrow loaded, and had a second arrow in his hand, ready to reload after firing the first.

Death stalking the forest has become Death lying in ambush, he chortled silently to himself. At this distance he never missed. As soon as he heard them reach the marsh grass and spotted a clear target, he would rise up like lightning itself and take his shot. Caught by total surprise, he doubted that his second target could duck and hide before he took a second, deadly shot. He supposed that they were armed, but probably only with pistols or revolvers, since he hadn't spotted either of them caring a rifle or any other long gun. He would have the advantage of range if any shootout actually occurred. All he had to do was be patient, and he was the best at that.

In the gradually fading light of the sunset in the forest, Angela still had no trouble picking out Junior's trail. She had been right. Although he still employed great skill in moving through the swamp, Junior was leaving small hints of tracks as he fled. Up ahead Danny and she could see more openness and light in the swamp, and as they moved in that direction, through the hemlocks, cedars and larch trees they saw the outlines of a beaver lodge rising up from marsh grass and dark, shallow water.

"Hold up a minute," Angela whispered.

"Do you see something? Is he up ahead?" Danny wondered, bringing his Ruger pistol up, ready for action.

"No," Angela answered, "but let's just look and wait a bit before we step out into any open place. He may have moved through and around that beaver lodge, but if he could be lying in wait, we don't want to give him an easy target."

Junior thought he heard his pursuers just inside the tree line at the edge of the marshy ground. It wasn't much, but he thought there was just a little slosh of water.

What are they doing? Why did they stop? Come on, you SOB's. Whatcha waiting for?

"Be alert," Angela whispered again. "Look all around."

And she bent over low and crept out into the marsh grass, moving toward the beaver lodge. Danny went with her, also bending over and scanning the area ahead of them as carefully as he could, swiveling his head at each slow step.

There! Junior saw his opportunity by raising his camouflaged head slightly. He planted his right foot in the mud and sticks of the lodge, pushed up to a crouching position, took quick but expert aim, and squeezed the trigger of his crossbow.

But at the very instant he touched off his shot, the Angel of Protection and Providence had Junior's foot impact some wetness that had been left by one of the beavers earlier that afternoon as it added an aspen branch to the top of the lodge. His boot sole slid in the slight muddiness, jolting him off-balance as he shot, and the bolt-like arrow zipped at high velocity past Danny's shoulder, burying its sharp point in the trunk of a cedar tree behind him.

In fast response, Danny raised his Ruger and squeezed off a shot at the camouflaged figure that skidded at the top of the beaver lodge. Danny was an excellent pistol shot at short ranges, but ironically the same slip that had ruined the crossbow shot also lurched Junior out of the way of Danny's bullet. Holding on to his precious crossbow, Junior's balance was completely lost, and he slid clumsily all the way down the backside of the beaver lodge.

Junior landed on his back in the shallow water and black, oozing muck of the marsh grass, but anxiously rolled over, staggered up, and high-stepped his way, with great splashing, to the far side of the little opening and into the dense trees and brush. Meanwhile, Danny and Angela crouched down, Danny craning his neck, desperately looking for another shot opportunity. They heard Junior splash away on the far side of the beaver lodge, and when they made their way around the side of it, they could hear him snapping branches as he barreled into the thick swamp.

Danny looked wide-eyed – fearful and ready at the same time – and clearly disappointed at Junior's escape.

"I should have had him," he moaned and apologized to Angela. "It was a good shot opportunity."

"This isn't all bad, either," she told him. "Again, he knows we can follow him wherever we have to. We're close on his trail, and we're not giving up. Besides, this is a good time to mark where we leave off and resume the pursuit tomorrow morning at first light. Meanwhile, not only will he have to rest during the night, but he'll do so covered in black muck, soaked to the skin."

"You're right," Danny felt lifted again by her encouragement. "We can be dry and warm tonight, but Junior Smith will have a very cold, damp, uncomfortable night." And they noted the coordinates in the cell phone of where they left the trail and headed back to the cabin.

CHAPTER TWENTY-SEVEN

Back at Uncle Jake's old cabin as twilight faded, Danny and Angela found it a proverbial beehive of activity. Bright lights were everywhere. State Police officers milled around, busying themselves with searching for evidence, examining the gear and supplies that had been piled up by the brothers to tote up to their hidden car, taking copious notes. Paramedics were attending to Crystal, having set up a temporary triage center in the main room of the cabin prior to carrying her on a stretcher up the little path to an ambulance that had bounced its way into the small parking space up on high ground. Andrea's Post Commander, Lieutenant Wade, was in the little cabin clearing, talking to and questioning Andrea and Tiny. Wes Smith was nowhere to be seen, but presumably was already handcuffed and placed in one of the several highway patrol cars that were parked, lights flashing, up on or by the two-track lane.

"Oh, good, you're back," Andrea instantly relaxed at the sight of Danny and Angela. "Lieutenant Wade was irate that two civilians were on the trail of the murderer of two state police officers and exposing themselves to danger."

"What about young Smith?" Lieutenant Wade barked, admittedly relieved that Danny and Angela were safe, but highly agitated about Junior's efforts to escape yet again.

Danny and Angela reported on their experience just then in tracking Junior to the little marshy clearing along the feeder creek, including the fact that he had attempted a shot at Danny with his crossbow. They had been too far away from the cabin for the low "pop" of Danny's return shot with the .22 pistol to be heard by the police there, but Lieutenant Wade asked if there was any chance he had hit Smith by returning fire.

"No, not a chance, I'm afraid," Danny admitted. "But he sure scrambled away as fast as he could go."

"Which way was he headed?" Wade wanted to know.

"North and west, or as far as we could tell, anyway. He should still be in the swamp, but probably closer by now to the Manistee River."

Lieutenant Wade and Andrea poured over a map book and their electronic satellite maps of the area. "If he keeps going in that general direction – and he's not about to double back in this direction – he'll have to make it across the river to keep going," Wade noted. "He wouldn't chance floating down the river. Too open. If he crosses the river...."

"Then he'd have to make it across West Sharon Road...maybe trying to reach the big East Lake Swamp surrounding Maple Creek," Andrea pointed.

"Our search teams will post all along West Sharon Road," Wade concluded. "We'll keep a chopper in the air over the river, just in case, and keep an eye there. And at first light we'll send dogs, handlers, and as many troopers as we can deploy, on his trail where you marked it for tonight. We'll get this cockroach if it's the last thing we do."

"What about the feds – the DEA and FBI agents due in Traverse City tomorrow morning?" Andrea asked.

"I wish they were here now to add to our forces," Lieutenant Wade admitted, "but I'm not waiting any longer than daylight tomorrow morning to get after this guy. Its two of our own that he's killed, and he will not get away again...not if I can do anything about it."

Angela, who had been standing nearby, but keeping quiet, spoke up. "Ah, Lieutenant, you remember me, I'm Angela Jones, used to be McGinty."

"Yah, sure, you were the other bride with Officer Henriks at the wedding. I stood up for both of you."

"You need to use me to track Smith tomorrow morning."

Wade tried to avoid any hint of condescension, but politely declined her offer. "We appreciate your efforts, Ms. Jones, we really do. We wouldn't know even where to start in the morning without your being after him this afternoon, but this is a police pursuit and capture, and we can't expose any of you to any more potential harm. Go home tonight, all three of you," looking at Angela, Tiny and Danny, "and leave it up to us now."

"I understand and totally respect your authority in this, Lieutenant, but as skilled and professional as your troopers and dog handlers are, they cannot follow his trail in this vast swamp. The dogs can't detect scent in all this water, and he won't leave the wet to give them better scenting conditions. Besides, he's as good as they come in navigating this forest wilderness. Danny, Andrea, tell him he needs me."

"It's true, sir," Danny chimed in. "Angela learned deep tracking as a girl in the Arizona Apache lands. I was with her this afternoon, and with all the tricks Smith has at his disposal, he could not shake her off his trail. The whole reason he tried to ambush us with his crossbow at the beaver lodge was that we were gaining on him. This woman knows what she's doing at levels no police officers get training in. Trust me on this. Trust her. What can it hurt? Even if you didn't think she could do it, you still have your search team and dogs to do their jobs."

"Yeah, Lieutenant," Andrea jumped in and hoped that she wasn't pressing so hard as to appear insubordinate, "what can it hurt to use Angela, too? It's not like she's going to throw anyone off Smith's trail. She can only help and give support to our efforts."

The Post Commander was open enough to listen and to consider what wisdom there may be in what they were arguing. "Okay, I'll fill in the brass above my head on this. If they don't put the kibosh on it, you be sure to be back here at this cabin tomorrow morning before first light, oh, say, no later than 7:00. There'll be search team people here all night, and I'll alert them that you'll be back in the morning, to let you through. Now all four of you – you, too, Officer Henriks – get back to Traverse City and get some rest. We capture this subject tomorrow."

They had been right about Junior Smith. He was soaked and covered with muck and mud. He didn't dare light even a small warming fire that night, with all the pursuers that were so close to him now. No matter. If anyone could tough it out in this swampy wilderness, it was he. He made his way to a large thicket on higher, drier ground. It was another spot frequented by bedding deer, and he found such a bed – an oval, depressed spot among the bushes filled with leaves. Shedding his backpack and setting down the dependable crossbow, he immediately set about gathering more dry leaves by armfuls, dumping them into the deer bed.

When he had a sizable mound of dry leaves filling the deer bed, he laid down in the leaves, literally wiggling his body back and forth, creating a nest around himself. Then he got up, slipped out of the thicket, snuck down the gentle slope a short way, and looked up at the thicket.

Nope, no piled-up leaves visible should anyone approach on my trail. That should do.

As the twilight faded to complete dark, he returned to his nest of leaves, crawled in, and pulled more of the leaves he had gathered in on top of himself. Even he was shivering a bit now from the combination of his wet clothes and the temperature in the swamp falling toward the freezing mark.

But one of the reasons he always insisted on wearing a thick, wool, camo shirt under his overalls was that even when wet, wool retained at least some of its insulating value. All of the air trapped in his leaf pile also created an insulating cocoon around him, and after a while he actually started to feel slightly warmer from his body heat being trapped in his nest with him. It wasn't like the cozy wood stove fire back at the old cabin, but he'd sleep warm enough to get through the night...and early tomorrow morning Death would resume stalking the forest and working out his getaway.

He just regretted that he hadn't put an arrow into that guy back at the beaver lodge. As he wiggled just a bit deeper in the leaves, he felt for the first time a slight twinge of pain in his left upper arm.

Funny how in the heat of things you can get bumps and bruises and not even realize it until after it's all over, he shrugged.

He drifted off to sleep without bothering to check on the small tear in his overall sleeve and the wool shirt sleeve under it...and the slight, red, .22 bullet crease in the skin of his left shoulder. He didn't even realize that one, two, three little drops of blood ran down his outer sleeve and fell on the leaves below him. Under different circumstances, it would have been a very minor matter with no particular consequences, but there are reasons they're called *bloodhounds*.

CHAPTER TWENTY-EIGHT

At precisely 7:00 Thursday morning, well before sunup, Andrea, Angela, Danny, and even Tiny were back at Uncle Jake's old log cabin. Danny and Tiny had no particular part to play now that the State Police had completely taken over the search and pursuit for Junior Smith, but Danny had insisted on driving his Grand Cherokee back to the cabin, and Tiny wasn't about to be left behind while the love of his life was tracking down a vicious murderer.

Lieutenant Wade was back, also, and was organizing both the tracking team and the outer net of officers who would contain the suspect if he tried to break out of his swampy hideout. He agreed to allow Andrea to be part of the tracking/pursuing team of officers, including two dog handlers with a German Shepherd and a purebred bloodhound. It was a very effective police dog team – the bloodhound was unparalleled in its ability to scent the smallest nano-bits of blood, skin, dander, hair, sweat...anything that made the faintest scent trail for its superb nose. The German Shepherd also had excellent tracking abilities, combined with training and experience in attacking and taking down dangerous human subjects.

Before 8:00, as the rising sun started to lighten the darkness of the swamp, the pursuit team – led by the two dogs, their handlers, and Angela – reached the coordinate where Angela and Danny had broken off tracking the night before. They picked up Junior's trail with no difficulty.

About a half-hour before – roughly 7:30 when the swamp was still dark – Junior had left his "deer bed" and headed back to the wet ground to resume his escape route. He had been super careful about his steps up to and down from his bedding spot, and while the super tracker who had been on his trail could probably figure it out, it should take longer and give him more of a head start. He knew that his meandering escape was taking him closer to the Big Manistee, and that sometime that morning he would have to decide whether to try to cross the river or navigate it upstream or down.

Angela, the handlers and the dogs readily found Junior's bed in the thicket. The leaves on the edges of his bedding area were coated with tell-tale frost. His body heat creeping out to the upper, outer leaves of his bedding cocoon condensed tiny amounts of moisture in the air just above the leaves. Those small traces of moisture on the outer leaves froze into white, crystalline needles of frost, roughly outlining part of his body shape in the leaves. And toward his upper body area in the leaf bed Angela spotted the tiny, but incredibly bright, red drops of blood. Simultaneously, the bloodhound sniffed at the area, raised its large muzzle, and howled in its deep, distinctive voice. The strike of the hot scent accelerated the pace of the pursuit as both dogs became agitated and strained to charge down the trail.

But as expected, Junior's trail was soon back in the wet

swamp where scent was washed away. Nonetheless, both the pursuers and the pursued felt pushed to pick up the pace. As the sun continued to rise gradually, the air temperature actually started to fall rather than rise as one would expect in the mid-morning. Small pellets of hard snow began to fall on the Northern Michigan forest. Junior cursed this development, as tiny, white snow pellets collecting in the slightest depressions left by his footprints would cause them to be easier to make out by even a mediocre tracker. He had to try another escape – or at least slowing – tactic.

He angled into some drier, but still soft, dark creek bottom soil and proceeded for some fifty yards or so. Then he halted, looked back at his faint, barely discernible tracks, and started to step *backwards*, ever so carefully and precisely into his own tracks. He had practiced this technique rigorously for years, like an Olympic athlete training for that premier competition that would be held four years ahead. Each step back into the next track behind him had to be exact, with not a slip or a smudge to disturb the original track. It took precious minutes to accomplish this backtracking, but he was the most disciplined any human could be about it, and it was perfectly done.

Roughly halfway back from where he had started on this soft soil, he reached his target spot – a large jumble of fallen logs he had skirted by. He had deliberately made a couple of steps closer to each other at that point than his normal stride. He paused, gathered his breath and relaxed his muscles, crouched down, and then like an Olympic high jumper, leaped into the air toward the logjam. He held his essential crossbow in his left hand, and at the top of his remarkable jump, he reached out with his wet glove on his right hand, caught the top log, and vaulted his entire body over and beyond the piled-up logs.

The result of this prodigious leap was that he left his trail, soared over the logs alongside his faint tracks, and landed with a jarring impact, but soundly, several yards away on the other side of the logjam. He gathered himself, shook his head, and then slipped away as lightly as he could possibly go in the wet swamp.

About fifteen minutes later, drawing inexorably closer to their quarry, Angela, the dogs, and the rest of the pursuit team came down his trail on the soft bottom soil of the creek bed.

Why, she wondered, *did he leave the wetness of the swamp water, where the dogs are much more challenged to pick up scent? Did he have some reason to want us to follow in this direction?*

Junior's tracks were almost invisible to virtually everyone who might be looking, but they stood out to Angela like beacons...and the dogs had no trouble detecting his scent, however slight it was with his wet boots.

Then the dogs and the handlers came to an abrupt stop.

"What's wrong? Why are we stopping?" Angela asked.

The dogs were whining and looking around, obviously confused about the trail. Andrea looked around, somehow hoping that she could spot something to help the pursuit.

"It's as though the trail just stops," one of the dog handlers said, perplexed. They prepared to start circling to pick it up again, which would take precious time, but he had to have gone somewhere. "He couldn't have risen straight up," the officer stated the obvious.

Angela bent over and examined the last tracks more closely. It dawned on her that she had gotten sloppy in her trailing, lulled into a less-engaged scrutiny by the relative ease of the trail and the energetic enthusiasm of the dogs and their humans.

"He didn't," she announced as she peered inches away from the last few tracks. "He's stepped backwards, very precisely, into each of his tracks behind him. I've never seen anyone do this so skillfully, but look, at each toe of his boots there's a very small, curved line in the soil marking the edge of the toe of the boot. As he lifts his foot to take another step, that edge of the boot sole makes a very small rub in the front curve of the track, sometimes causing a few grains of soil to fall into the track. Now each of the tracks that are visible should have that tiny, minor disturbance of grains of soil, but there's no particular reason for the same phenomenon to occur at the back of the boot track. The boot should lift pretty cleanly most of the time out of the track."

"Now look at these tracks, however. No matter how precisely he's put his foot back into the old track behind him, when he lifts his foot to step backward again, the edge of his heel catches ever so slightly the lip of the track, and sometimes causes grains of soil to crumble around and into the re-formed track. He's walked backward.... right to this point," and she pointed to the jumbled logs piled up next to the trail.

The dogs sniffed around the logjam – the German Shepherd showing interest in the logs up high, and the bloodhound working nose to the ground around to the far side of the pile. Finally, the hound caught hot scent and bayed again its excitement. Angela, the handlers, Andrea and the other officers with them, all took off with increased energy in the new direction.

About 20 minutes ahead of the pursuers Junior paused and listened to the baying of the hound. Obviously, they were hard on his trail again. He hoisted himself up on a leaning cedar trunk where he could look back and down in the direction in which he had come. Screened by the cedar branches, he kept listening, and after a while could hear both the dogs, their handlers giving commands, and every now and then Angela's voice, announcing another find in the trail they were unraveling.

Who is this woman? Junior wondered. *My little backtracking maneuver should have delayed them a good half-hour – maybe extend my lead on them to a good hour – and she sorts it out in five minutes? Even my Injun tracker buddy Simon Deerfoot isn't that good. How's she doing it? I need another delaying tactic.*

He wasn't panicking, and he still had full confidence in his woods craft, but a rising, nagging concern welled up that was strange to him.

He envisioned the shrinking expanse of swamp that still lay ahead of him. Meanwhile, the hard, little snow pellets were continuing to fall, scattering a thin white cover over the surface of the swamp. Anywhere he went now would show sloppy tracks in the dusting of snow.

Damn, he swore to himself, *it's not fair that everyone is against me, now goddamned Mother Nature is, too.*

He reached the big boulder that incongruously sat at the edge of another hillock, an unusual deposit left by the last glacier to have covered the area thousands of years ago.

A sharp wind out of the north, carrying the swirling snow pellets, had kept the top of the boulder bare. It was another move of desperation, but in a spontaneous attempt to buy whatever time he could and somehow extend his lead on this mysterious tracker woman, Junior made a long leap to the lower half of the boulder, jumped to the top of the higher half, and steadied himself. He stepped back as far as he could on the top of the great rock, took two quick steps forward, and launched himself down the slight slope into the brush and brambles below.

His landing involved numerous scrapes and scratches, but the thicket also cushioned his fall and once again he gathered himself, crouched where he had come to a stop, and looked back. His tracks would have led right to the boulder, but then stopped. He hoped that he had left no evidence on the rough surface of the big rock, but he knew that his jump had carried him maybe as much as 15 feet away from the far side of the boulder. He knew it wouldn't stop the pursuit, but maybe it would take a longer time for them to figure out where he went this time. He couldn't afford to linger, however, so he pressed on, with the Big Manistee not far ahead.

CHAPTER TWENTY-NINE

Angela, Andrea and the pursuit team reached the giant boulder. The trail seemed to lead right to it, so they slowed up, guns drawn, in case he was hiding on the other side of the rock like he did at the beaver lodge. They eased closer, restraining the dogs, and when they got to the boulder, once more it seemed as though the tracks had disappeared. There weren't even any prints in the gradually accumulating light snow on the ground.

"Well," Andrea concluded, "again we know he didn't go straight up. But this time he couldn't have leaped over this boulder. Besides, there aren't any tracks anywhere around it."

"Spiral," Angela said abruptly.

"What?" puzzled one of the dog handlers.

"Spiral," she repeated. "Take the dogs and we'll all go around this boulder in a gradually-widening spiral. Since he didn't step backward in his own tracks, he had to have leapt off of the boulder and landed hard not too far away. A spiraling search pattern is the quickest way to regain the trail."

She was right, of course, and only the second loop of the spiral found his landing place in the thick brush, along with the new trail he made as he took off again. They picked up their pace, since they had a freshly made trail to work, and they had to be closing in on him.

Their catching up to him was a fact that was not lost on Junior. The woman and the dogs were hard on his trail, and nothing he tried was throwing them off...nor even slowing them down. To make matters worse, his hard landing jumping off the boulder had tweaked his left ankle. It was not serious, but he knew he couldn't run fast or be as nimble after that. There was only one more possibility before he reached the river and would be forced to use or cross the Manistee.

He had relied heavily on his use of the swamps and creeks to eliminate scent for dogs and to make human pursuit arduous and ineffective. Less than a mile to the river there was a virtually impenetrable patch of balsam swamp. It was full of thick cedars, too, but the balsams grew with their low-sweeping, scratchy, needle-filled branches right down to ground level. Even the deer didn't use the balsam swamp very much, since it was so hard to get around in. Occasionally he had hiked that far from the cabin and set traps and nooses around the edges and a little way into the balsams to snare snowshoe hares, which loved the place for the great protection it provided from their primary predators.

He hated the thought of having to struggle deep into the balsam swamp, but to his surprise and dismay, nothing else had worked. At least if he forced his way into the center of it, he could catch his panting breath, think, and figure out the next best step and place to flee to. He sucked it up and pushed into the interlocking, tearing balsam boughs. Three steps and anyone right behind him wouldn't have been able to see him anymore.

Andrea, Angela, and their pursuit partners were only about ten minutes behind when the no-longer disguised trail headed into the balsams. They, too, stopped and considered how to proceed. The hardworking dogs scurried back and forth at the edge of the balsam swamp, sniffing at the hot tracks that disappeared into the wall of foliage.

Andrea phoned back to the field headquarters at the old cabin and reported on the situation. "We're hot behind him, sir," she informed Lieutenant Wade. "It's going to be hard to chase him down in these balsams and cedars, but we're catching our breath, giving the dogs and ourselves water, and we'll go in and get him."

"In the meantime," he replied, "we've been reinforced by DEA and FBI, as well as more of our troopers from downstate. If you want to hold up, we could surround the whole balsam patch with law enforcement, fly the chopper down low over it, and use the loudspeaker to demand that he give up on a hopeless situation."

"Negative, sir," she replied, "this can't be his end game. He's been unable to lose us from his trail, and I'm sure that he's just buried himself in here to buy time for his next move. He can only go to the river, up it, down it, or cross it, which would leave him highly exposed in any of those options. I think we need to move in and not give him any more time to come up with any other plan. He's wet. He has to be tired. He couldn't have gotten a good night's sleep, and his tracks indicate a bit of a limp in his left leg. I don't think we should let up on him."

"Okay, Henriks, you're the one on the scene. Keep up the pressure, but if he resists and you can't get him to surrender, it's deadly force if you have to use it."

"Roger, sir," she understood and agreed. "We'll make every effort to take him alive, but it's up to him." She turned to the pursuit team, "Angela, you can stay out here with Officer Olson – his German Shepherd has a cut pad – but the rest of us are going in. Visibility is almost nil in there, so be extra vigilant and make sure you don't present an easy target for his crossbow."

CHAPTER THIRTY

Andrea and the dog handler with the bloodhound pushed their way into the balsams on Junior's clearly visible tracks. Sharp needles and stiff branches snapped at their faces and necks as they tried to hold the boughs open to proceed. Andrea bent low under a sweeping bough and immediately had cold snow dumped down the back of her neck. Then she had to clamber over crisscrossed logs on the ground, over which hung more low branches, so that she was sharply doubled over, straining to be able to see ahead and try to make sure that she was not presenting herself as that easy target.

Her primary consolation in this crazy hunt for the desperate murderer was the realization that it had to be just as difficult – maybe even more so – for him to get anywhere in this balsam swamp. The bloodhound and his handler had to give up and ease their way back out. It was just too thick for the poor dog to be effective. Besides, there was no longer anything subtle about the trail. There were no more tricks, no more elusive strategy, and no more woods craft to confound the less expert in the forest. The pursuit had slowed and ground its way into an endurance contest. The only question that really remained was whether Junior would face up to the futility of his efforts to escape and surrender...or whether Andrea and her pursuit team would wear him down and subdue him.

Junior had been surprised again by the determination and skill of his pursuers. He had been confident that confronted by the almost impenetrable balsam patch those infernal women on his trail would back off and wait for reinforcements. If they weren't so cussedly stubborn, he would have his time to stop, think, and plan his next move. But no, they had to keep coming.

And they're just women, he complained to himself. *Who are these, these Amazons, these Harpies from the dark pages of mythology, these Valkyries chasing him down? God, why does the whole female race plague him so unfairly?*

He had never known a man, or men, who could keep up with him in the deep forest. *Why don't they quit?*

He slumped down behind a large, decaying, moss-covered balsam log lying on the floor of the swamp. His ankle was throbbing now with all of the exertion he had been forced to make. *Time to switch from defense to offense again,* he decided, and placed an arrow in the track of his crossbow. *Come on, bitch. You're so damned determined to get me, well, come and try.* He placed the cocked, camo-painted crossbow on top of the log and took aim. All that stuck up above the curve of the log was the crossbow and his camo hat. *She can't see me, and she'll never know what hit her.* He gritted his teeth and waited, the ultimate Predator in the forest.

Andrea held her left forearm in front of her face to push

through the scratching boughs of the balsams. She had to keep her right hand free to be able to fire her gun as needed. For the umpteenth time she tripped over a dead log on the needle-covered ground. She almost burst out into a little bit of an opening among the dense trees...and there he was, taking aim.

Junior's patience and discipline finally paid off. He could hear and see his pursuer pushing through the boughs on his trail. He didn't wait any longer than he had to. As soon as he got a good image of the body mass parting the branches, he fired.

The arrow shot like a bullet to its target, striking with brutal force and sending his victim toppling over backwards into the dense boughs and down to the ground.

Yah! he rejoiced triumphantly to himself. *Take that, bitch.*

CHAPTER THIRTY-ONE

J unior wasn't about to wait for the other pursuers to rally and come after him. He wasn't sure if he had shot that demon tracker that had relentlessly trailed him to this point...or the female cop who was with her. He just took the shot as soon as it was available, and then he took off as well as he could, squeezing among the dense balsam and cedar trees. *That should slow them down enough for me to get out of here,* he felt with renewed confidence. *It'll take all of them to carry her body through that dense patch that a damned rabbit can hardly negotiate. And I'll be on my way to escaping, finally.* Within another 20 minutes he had reached the far side of the infernal balsams and came almost within view of the Big Manistee River ahead of him.

Andrea froze for a split-second at the sight of Junior hunkered down behind the log, aiming his crossbow. Her head turned to the left as he took his shot, and she saw Trooper Benson topple backwards into the interlocking branches that he was just pushing through. She had put him on Junior's tracks, following step-by-step through the dense foliage, but since there was no space for several pursuers to be on the trail, she had sent Trooper Harding to flank closely off to the left of the trail, while she made the same parallel flanking movement on the right of Junior's tracks. It was pure coincidence that she reached the narrow opening just in time to see him take aim and fire.

With amazing speed, Junior had risen, stepped back in the same motion, and melted into the trees behind him. Andrea would have gotten a shot at him, but her attention had been diverted by Trooper Benson being knocked backward by the crossbow arrow.

"Benson!" she hollered as Junior crashed noisily through the balsams, desperate to get out of there. She fought her way over to her fallen trooper, fearful of his life, but felt just a small bit of relief that he was kicking, grabbing the spot up on his right shoulder where the arrow had struck, and moaning with pain. It was serious, and he'd need immediate first aid, starting with stopping the blood flow as best they could, but the arrow had missed his lung and hadn't struck any major artery. She opened his field jacket, took clean cloths and pressed around the wound site to staunch the bleeding.

"Harding, over here," Andrea called to the other flanker, and soon he fought his way to her and the panting Benson. "I'll stay with him, but fight your way out of here and get Jackson and the first-aid kit, ASAP." And before he even left, she called Jackson to let him know he and his paramedic skills were needed.

As Harding pushed through the trees to do just that, Andrea used her free hand to make the "officer down" call and report on this latest development to her commander.

"Is Benson going to be okay? Dispatch is sending a medical evac helicopter to land as close to you as we can figure out," Lieutenant Wade assured her.

"Roger that, sir, the arrow is sticking in his upper right shoulder. It has to hurt like hell..." to which Benson nodded, gritting his teeth in his pain. "But he should be okay so long as we keep the blood loss at a minimum."

"Well, you better break off the pursuit and back out of there. We'll flush the suspect out another way."

"Negative, sir," Andrea called back. "We've caught up to him. He's slowing down, and the direction he took is going to have him at the Manistee River in a matter of minutes. You can order me to break off, sir, and of course I will, but if we keep the pressure on, he'll be forced out of here and have to deal with the river ahead of him."

After a second's pause, the commander agreed. "And I can order the chopper over the river to keep watch as he reaches it. I'll have a lot more reinforcements blanket both sides of the river, up and down from where you are. There's no way he'll be able to get away. But don't expose yourself or the rest of the pursuit team to any more of his crossbow fire, you got it? Pressure him, but don't get too close, and that's an order."

"Affirmative, sir," Andrea obeyed. "We'll make sure he doesn't double back behind us, but I won't let him pick off any more troopers, not by a damn sight."

In about ten minutes somehow Harding was back with Jackson and the first-aid kit. It wouldn't have been possible to fight through the dense trees and back that quickly, save for the fact that Andrea had called Jackson to let him know to come running...or more accurately, crawling, scrambling, fighting through the dense swamp. The obvious initial treatment was to immobilize the arrow as best they could, pack the wound site, administer pain killers, leave it sticking in his shoulder – probably until the ambulance could transport him to the emergency room at Kalkaska – and clear a path as well as possible to get him out of there.

If it didn't endanger him or threaten to make the wound worse, it would be easier if he could walk out with support on each side. But if that wasn't possible or best for him, he would have to be taken out by stretcher, no easy feat in that hellish environment. Junior had been right in his strategy. He had shot to kill, of course, but as is usually the case on any battlefield, wounding was often better to gain advantage over the enemy. A kill shot eliminated one of your enemies, but a serious wound could take out the victim, a couple of stretcher bearers, a medic, sometimes even more, away from the fight.

In either case, Junior thought grimly that Death was still stalking the forest and would prevail. *That last shot in the density of the balsam patch should put a halt to the pursuit for the time being.* He slipped underneath the low-sweeping branches of yet another cedar tree, where he was invisible in his camo, and looked out on the dark, heavy current of the Big Manistee about 30 yards ahead of him. He waited, watched, and kept to his disciplined woods craft. A truly expert woodsman exercised patience and struck when the time was exactly right...whether it was a deer as a target, or a stupid pig of a cop, or a bitch in uniform, or just a river escape that was needed. And he had a plan now for that.

CHAPTER THIRTY-TWO

Andrea made the command decision on the field that it was too strenuous and risky for Trooper Benson to try to walk through the balsam jungle, but his bleeding had slowed, pain was eased, and he seemed stable enough to be able to wait for stretcher bearers. Leaving his bloodhound with the German Shepherd's handler and Angela, the second dog handler pushed into the balsams to be with Jackson and Benson.

"Come on, Harding," Andrea hissed through her clenched teeth, "Let's not give this bastard any time to rest and recover." She knew that he had put a good deal more stress on his strained ankle, and little drag marks were starting to show in the tracks Junior made in the light snow cover. He was favoring that ankle.

"Stay a few yards to the left of his trail," Andrea ordered, "and I'll stay to the right, but stick close and don't fall behind. I don't want either of us to lag behind and provide another single target for him to aim at."

Even though there were now just two state police troopers pushing forward on his trail, at least Andrea and Harding outnumbered the murderer two-to-one. And although he had more than demonstrated his lethality with his crossbow, they were well-armed with handguns and the rifle that Harding carried, set for short bursts of fire. So long as they avoided another of his ambushes, they had him considerably outgunned.

Junior kept watching and waiting, and his patience and discipline was finally rewarded. A Michigan State Police helicopter swooped over the river in front and above him, slowly scanning the water and the banks on either side. When it was well past him and out-of-sight, he knew it was time to put his plan into action. But then he heard Trooper Harding knock over a leaning, dead fir tree back in the balsam swamp as he tried to brush past it. Junior's best guess was that the sound was no more than 50-75 yards behind him on his trail. He had to act quickly. There would only be one try, succeed or fail, get away or be captured.

He had deliberately come out to the river in the thick woods alongside a river-front cottage. Having hiked unseen by the place before, he remembered that the owners kept an Old Town, 15-foot canoe turned over on the high bank above the river. Since the people had not yet put everything away for winter storage, he smiled when he saw that it was still there.

On the next pass over the river, the helicopter spotter saw the canoe drifting downstream in the heavy, main current. Training his binoculars on the canoe as it seemed to drift unguided, he saw that its interior was mostly covered with an old, canvas tarp, but he spotted the soles of boots sticking out of the tarp to the stern end of the canoe. Shifting his view slowly up to the bow, he also spotted a camouflaged glove sticking out from under the tarp, clutching the starboard gunwale of the canoe, as though someone was trying to brace against the canoe banging into logs in the water as it drifted downstream to the west.

"I have a visual," the spotter announced both to his pilot and into his radio for command to hear. "It appears to be an occupied canoe, drifting loosely downstream, with a subject hiding under a canvas tarp in the bottom of the craft."

"We have him," Lieutenant Wade announced into his mike. "All units converge on the coordinates I'm about to give you." The helicopter, of course, kept a tight circle above the drifting canoe, which would sometimes lodge briefly against logs and brush, and then be spun free to continue downstream.

Andrea and Trooper Harding emerged from the balsam and cedar tangle just a moment too late to see the canoe leave the bank outside the unoccupied cottage, but it wasn't long before they got the commander's radio message. Andrea stood unmoving, however, and looked slowly and carefully at the river, the cottage, and as best she could, at the surrounding forest.

"Henriks," Trooper Harding spoke, "we need to respond. The lane into this cottage will take us out to West Sharon Road, and we can join up with a patrol car there."

"Just hold on a minute, Harding," she replied. "Lieutenant," she spoke into her radio, "Harding and I are still by the cottage where our suspect seems to have commandeered that canoe. There are drag marks down to the water's edge and his boot tracks. But do you have a status report on Angela Jones?"

Just a bit annoyed at the distraction, but respecting the question of one of his best officers, the field commander replied, "When they got Benson out of that swamp, she went in a patrol car out to South Sharon Road. They drove north to our checkpoint at the Sharon crossroads, where her husband and yours are waiting. Copy?"

"Copy that. Would you have the officer driving the car she's in bring her here to this cottage? I need her tracking ability."

"Why?" the Lieutenant demanded, fatigue and exasperation in his voice. "You don't think the perpetrator is in that canoe?"

"He's given us the slip before, sir. I just want to make sure."

It wouldn't hurt for him to humor her, and she was right about the elusiveness of this younger Smith brother, so he had the message sent, and then turned his focus back to the forces converging on the canoe.

When officers with guns drawn, barking commands, caught up to the canoe drifting clumsily downstream, the suspect refused to show his hands – other than the one clutching the gunwale – and refused to get up and surrender. Finally, four officers, two on each side, waded around the canoe in the frigid water, and on a three-count, two grabbed the edges of the canvas tarp and pulled hard, while the other two kept their weapons ready to fire at the least sign of a threat.

What they uncovered was a stick wedged under the front seat of the canoe, holding the otherwise empty glove in place on the gunwale, and two empty boots that had been sticking just outside the back of the tarp. One of the soles had a small, wedge-shaped chunk torn out of the outside tread. It would match the one clear print found at Trooper Baldwin's body on the highway.

"He's not here in the damn canoe," an officer sputtered into his radio. "It was a diversion. We don't know where he is." Dozens of state troopers, FBI and DEA agents, and support personnel groaned in frustration and anger, and the frantic search was back on, heading back upstream on the river.

Meanwhile, two state troopers delivered Angela to the cottage as ordered, but both they and Trooper Harding were highly irritated that they were being forced to stay "out of the action." Understandably, they had all wanted to be on or near the scene when the scumbag murderer was apprehended. Andrea recognized their frustration at what they felt was being put "on the sideline," but she didn't have the luxury of time to explain and to try to make them feel better about their restriction.

"Ang," she brightened as she saw her best friend get out of the patrol car. "I need you to examine the apparent launch spot and tell me what you see."

Angela followed her quickly over to the groove in the sand where Junior had obviously pushed the canoe into the current. In what the other officers present felt was a waste of time and resources, she scrutinized the area, even getting down on all fours and peering into the shallow water at the sandy bottom near the bank.

Finally, she got up and turned specifically to Andrea, "There are small indentations in the sand on the bottom. The eddying back current is gradually washing them away, but you can just barely see that he was standing there in the shallows in his bare feet. Out a little way there's a stronger depression that probably marks where he planted his foot to push off the canoe. The groove marking the keel and bottom of the canoe is faint, suggesting that there was little weight when it launched...probably empty. My best guess is that he was never in the canoe, and certainly not when it started its drift downstream."

The two officers who had brought her looked silently at each other, one lifting his eyebrow like, *Really, who does she think she's fooling?* But Harding stepped closer to see what she was talking about. He had been with her through the swamp as one of the pursuit team, and she had amazed him more than once before.

"Where did he head, then?" Andrea asked, anxious that he was slipping away yet again.

Angela turned to face upstream. "There are no tracks whatsoever along this bank. It would be unlike him to leave an obvious trail at this point, since he's trying to sell his canoe diversion. He had to have waded barefoot out into the river. He wouldn't have gone downstream, following the canoe, since he would want to create as much distance as possible between himself and the searchers converging on the canoe. He wouldn't wade back into dry land very soon, because he wouldn't want any fresh tracks to be spotted, even by accident, with us milling around here. Best guess again is that he waded some distance upstream in this cold water and swift current before he left the river. He wouldn't wait too long to get out, however, because wading in the stream exposes him out in the open."

Andrea took her analysis as pure gospel. Harding nodded affirmatively, everything she said ringing true to his ears. The other two officers looked again at each other, changing their expressions to ones of respect and being impressed. Following close behind Angela, the four state troopers headed along the bank, guns at the ready, and worked their way upstream. About thirty yards into the surrounding forest, she spotted a dead branch sticking from the bank down into the shallow water, and it had obviously been shoved aside, leaving a mark in the streamside sandy mud.

Angela crept over to the branch and spotted just the outside heel mark of Junior's bare foot in the sand. The pursuit was on again.

CHAPTER THIRTY-THREE

Junior Smith had just enough time to take the tarp off the overturned canoe, roll it over upright, take off his boots and arrange them and his remaining glove under the tarp inside the canoe so that it looked from above as though he was hiding under the tarp. He waded out into the stream a few feet, pushed hard, and launched the canoe out into the main current. He then waded quickly upstream and hugged the shoreline until he found a good, thick place to exit the water. His slipping into the dense brush literally occurred at the same moment that Andrea and Trooper Harding emerged from the balsam swamp and moved into the "yard" around the streamside cottage.

Hearing them so close behind him raised his bothersome anxiety. He had been convinced that shooting one of those bitches would create a longer interruption in the police pursuit. *Will they never let up? Who is this woman? This relentless persecution is just unfair. They're always against me,* he cursed to himself.

If he had a mirror to look into just then, he would have cursed how they had worn him to a proverbial frazzle. He was still damp all over from the previous day and today's desperate chase. Despite his woods craft in making his own "deer bed" for the night, he had been chilled during the cold night and never really warmed with the slow, excruciating pace of the hunt for him. He had fled the cabin, leaving his older brother behind, without being able to grab any food or drink. And despite Wes telling him to do so, it bothered him and he fretted about deserting his big brother. Both his warm, camo gloves and his boots were gone now, discards during his attempts to throw his pursuers off his track. He still had his trusted crossbow, but his arrow supply had dwindled with the ones he had shot and a couple that had been knocked off the arrow holder by having to fight through the most god-awful thick stuff in the wettest swamps he knew. He considered himself to be in top condition, able to stalk through the forest for miles each day, but more than once during this pursuit he had been panting for breath, especially with what was clearly a sprained ankle. The camo design he had painted on his face the previous day had been largely rubbed and worn off, being replaced by numerous red, irritating scratches, bruises and small cuts. His eyes were bloodshot, and one was partially closed by a hard smack from a balsam bough.

Worse than any other wear and tear, he *knew*, without a doubt, that he was the best in the woods. He was without par as a hunter and trapper. He was the ultimate Predator. He really *was* Death stalking in the forest. Everybody who knew him was in awe of his woods craft and especially his ability to disappear seemingly at will, not to be found unless he wanted it so. And yet, he had somehow become the prey, chased and worn down as if on his heels were the very hounds of hell. He believed that he had taken one of the witches out of the pursuit, but still the other one closed on him. *Who is this woman? Maybe she really is a witch, to have that kind of power to undo me.*

Junior was totally unaccustomed to being plagued by such doubts and fears. His wide eyes scoured the woods around him. He shook off the feeling that he was surrounded by demons in blue uniforms by literally shaking his head full of long, matted hair. *Well, they don't have me yet,* he actually ground his teeth together in trembling rage. He began to envision a last stand upstream somewhere, gallantly firing off crossbow arrows as they rushed him from all sides, firing a hail of bullets. He would be Custer at the Little Bighorn, John Dillinger in Chicago. He shook his head again even more violently. *Am I hallucinating now? What's wrong with me? I have to pull myself together. I can still get out of this. The canoe ruse will throw them off for a while. It will create some time and distance. All I need is to draw at least some of them away from West Sharon Road, and then hijack a passing car.*

But as he shivered from his emergence from the river moments ago, he heard Angela, Andrea, and her state troopers, working through the streamside brush in his direction. *They didn't even bite on my canoe diversion? I spent more time setting that up than they spent dismissing it. And now they're even closer. Hounds from hell led by witches.* Without the time available to worry about hiding his trail, Junior took off in virtually a panic, stumbling and falling in his brush-busting, no longer the ghost gliding through the forest.

He now made such a commotion that Angela, Andrea, and the troopers heard him not far ahead in the woods. They picked up the pace as Andrea called in their hot pursuit to field command center. In little more than a quarter of a mile, Junior came to the next cottage on the river frontage. Still trying to think of some place to hide, or to fight, or to do *something*, he ran, limping, around to the far side of the cottage. Like others on the river, the downstate owners had been winding down the summer/fall season at their place in the woods, and since it was Thursday, they had it closed and locked-up until they came up for the weekend Friday night. But few people in the area had much in the way of security, and Junior quickly broke a pane of glass in the side door facing their detached garage, turned the knob, and let himself in.

He tried to maintain the delusion that maybe his close pursuers would rush on by, not realizing that he had broken into the cottage, and that when they charged into the woods on the other side, he could slip out again and double back. But his rational thinking still wrestled with his anxious feelings and wild hopes, and he forced himself to face up to the fact that if they could track him and catch up to him in the wet swamps and the wild forest...they would surely have no difficulty finding him in a fancy riverfront cottage.

He had no choice but to try again to pick off at least one of his pursuers, to try again to get them to back off and give him a fighting chance to slip away. Rather than hole up in the cottage and wait for them to surround and toss in tear gas...or whatever they might do...he decided to go back out the door with the broken pane, jump off the porch so that his wet, barefoot tracks would only be seen going in, and hide in the unlocked garage only a few yards away from that door. He was pleasantly surprised with what he found in the garage.

CHAPTER THIRTY-FOUR

Andrea and her officers reached the edge of the rough lawn around the cottage, where she called a temporary halt to deploy.

"Our orders are to contain the subject, but to be cautious about giving him any more targets to shoot at," she reminded Trooper Harding and the two officers who had brought Angela to her. "Ang, please stay back here and stay safe, okay?" Angela nodded and obeyed.

Andrea positioned one of the officers to the left, to post between the cottage and the river, watching the patio doors and the deck overlooking the riverfront. The other she sent to circle around to the far side of the cottage and garage, blocking any further flight on the part of Junior in the direction he had been heading.

"Harding," she ordered, "come with me. We're going to check out the doors to the cottage and watch the drive going from the garage out to the county road. Angela," she called back, "stay put, but give a holler if you should see the bastard slip by us and double-back the way we came. But do not, you hear me, do not approach or confront him. The last thing we need is another hostage situation. If we can get a fix on just where he is here, we'll guard our perimeter and wait for reinforcements to arrive and flush him out."

Having surrounded the scene as best she could, Andrea moved forward cautiously, scanning from side to side, gun at the ready, looking for any movement or sign of where Junior had gone or holed up. There were absolutely no indications that he had gone up to the front porch and door, no tracks in the grass or on the flagstone walk.

With Harding on her hip, backing her up, Andrea moved around to the far side of the cottage to the side door. Harding hissed at her, "Look, up there on the side porch, that pane has been busted in, and there are shards of glass on the porch. He's in there, waiting to ambush us."

As Harding strained to peer in the windows of the cottage, Andrea ordered him back, "Just hold on, trooper, we're not to approach, remember? And what about the garage? We haven't checked that out yet. Let's eliminate possibilities first."

Trooper Harding nodded his assent and backed away from the cottage. Andrea posted him several yards in front of the garage door, and then moved very carefully toward the side door facing the cottage, reaching out with her left hand to turn the knob as quietly as possible, while holding her service pistol at the ready in her right hand.

Inside the garage, Junior had searched quickly and found the keys for the ATV conveniently hanging on a pegboard just inside the side door. He set his crossbow down on the front passenger seat, inserted the ignition key, and his luck continued as he found a garage door opener under the driver's seat. He grabbed the crossbow, held it firmly with the butt of the stock in the hollow of his right arm, his trigger finger resting on the trigger, ready to fire as soon as he burst out through the garage door. He turned the key first, and was rewarded with the little engine catching right away. He pressed the opener, and the garage door rose. He revved a little bit, then as soon as he had enough clearance, shifted into drive and gunned the ATV forward.

At the sound of the ATV's motor starting up and the garage door rising, Andrea released the side door handle and sprinted to the front corner of the garage. Trooper Harding, meanwhile, was bending over, trying to get a target acquired as soon as the garage door rose far enough for him to be able to see the ATV. Spotting Junior behind the wheel, he took aim, but Junior was ready and quicker. He let go his shot with the crossbow. Fortunately for Harding, his shooting stance had him twisted partly sideways, his left foot forward. The crossbow arrow sped across the front of his trooper's jacket, close under his chin, tearing a gash in the jacket material and knocking the pull tab off his jacket zipper as it shot by. A fraction of an inch change in any direction would have buried it in his chest cavity. As it was, the close miss caused Harding to stumble backwards and he didn't get his shot off.

As the ATV hurtled forward toward the doorway, Andrea spotted a wheeled trash bin standing at the front corner of the garage, ready to roll out to the county road for the weekly pickup. Reacting like lightning, she pushed the trash bin as hard as she could toward the accelerating ATV as it reached the doorway.

Under other circumstances, the wheeled trash bin would probably have struck the right front corner of the ATV, but had little more effect than giving it a jolt and spinning away to fall over. But God's will is expressed in concrete actions strictly according to God's time, at the *right and necessary* time. The Angel tipped the trash bin over exactly in front of the ATV's wheels, causing the off-road vehicle to lurch up on the side of the bin, tip sideways as the drive wheels kept churning, and fall over on the driver's side.

Trooper Harding's gaze sped from his torn jacket to the ATV and tipped trash bin to Andrea as she charged around the bin and the ATV, holding her gun at Junior's bleeding head lying on the driveway, his legs pinned under the little vehicle.

Andrea stepped forward, planted her left boot on Junior's neck and barked at him forcefully, "You so much as twitch, dirt bag, and it'll be the last move you ever make on earth."

Junior Smith narrowed his eyes as he glared at her, "Who *are* you, lady?"

"I'm your worst nightmare, kid. I'm God's Avenging Angel and your time is up. Give me a reason, and you'll meet your Maker right now."

Junior closed his eyes and shut up. God's true Avenging Angel took no note, let alone offense, at Andrea's impersonation. Angels are solely agents of God's plan, will, and work in this created universe. If the Angel had possessed human-like thoughts and emotions, it might have smiled and nodded appreciation at Andrea's victory. Divine justice had acted, and evil had been thwarted.

Both human and divine judgment still lay ahead for Junior and Wes Smith, and the Final Judgment to come would be far starker and more incomprehensible to mere mortals than words can ever express. Humans were fond of creating images, metaphors, and similes for both Heaven and Hell, but even biblical streets of gold and lakes of burning fire were trivial to an extreme in the face of the cosmic reality. There is simply no way even to hint at the perfection of being United with God for eternity...nor the absolute Separation of being without God for eternity.

Andrea's fellow officers and Angela crowded around the

ATV, congratulating her and securing the scene. Death as represented by Junior Smith no longer stalked anywhere.

CHAPTER THIRTY-FIVE

Andrea could scarcely believe the utter exhaustion that swept over her with the release of the stress and tension of the pursuit...and the relaxation of her mind, muscles, and spirit now that Junior Smith was in custody. As soon as the promised reinforcements arrived and she was relieved at the capture scene, a car took Angela and her to the Sharon crossroads where Danny and Tiny were waiting, along with the field commander, Lieutenant Wade.

Wade opened the door for Andrea to get out.

"Congratulations, officer, job well done," he smiled and shook her weary hand.

"Thank you, sir," Andrea replied wearily. "Give credit to the pursuit team and to the fantastic tracking job done by Angela Jones."

"You have our eternal gratitude and utmost respect, Ms. Jones," Wade agreed, shaking Angela's hand also as she came around the back of the patrol car. "I'll have more to say to both of you later, but right now I think you have a couple of gentlemen callers," he grinned.

Simultaneously Danny wrapped his arms around Andrea, not caring how unprofessional their embrace might look to her colleagues, and Tiny enveloped Angela in one of his patented bear hugs, lifting her off the pavement like a rag doll.

"Wow," Danny exclaimed, "I was never so worried in all my life. But what a job you did, hon." He leaned over to whisper in her ear: "I overheard your name and 'medal for bravery' mentioned in the same sentence already."

"Let's not get ahead of things," she demurred. "The important thing is that we got the SOB, and he'll pay for the murder of two state police officers and the critical wounding of a third...as well as kidnapping and assault of Crystal Johnson."

In their own ardent embrace, Tiny kept telling Angela how much he loved her, and how proud he was of the way she tracked down this super woodsman.

"I never knew you had that level of skill," he smiled with an additional measure of respect and appreciation for this amazing woman he had married. "Maybe the Michigan State Police will retire all their canine cops and give you a full-time career tracking down the bad guys."

"Oh, no," she protested. "I was glad to help this time – especially to help our Andrea – but it will be back to the gift shop and my bookkeeping for this girl. This chasing a murderer through the trackless forest is exhausting, hard work. I'll leave the apprehension of criminals up to the true professionals."

Lieutenant Wade was standing nearby and heard Angela's words to Tiny.

"Well, we couldn't have done it without you, Ms. Jones," he said with complete sincerity. "Perhaps you'd allow us to call you in once in a while as a consultant in tough tracking cases...for an appropriate fee, of course."

"Fees," Tiny gave his biggest grin, "I like the sound of that, sugar." His entrepreneurial wheels started turning, "Could be an additional feature in *Tiny's Big Protection Services.*"

Angela shot him a "Gee, thanks for opening your big mouth" look, and smiled at Lieutenant Wade, "Call me if ever you need me, Lieutenant, but you won't offend me if I don't hear from you again about having to track down a murderer."

The commander in the field turned back to Andrea, "Trooper Henriks, you and the rest of your pursuit team need some rest, food and hot coffee. I'll have the booking of your collar taken care of back at the post, and you can worry about your report and other paperwork when you report in tomorrow. Call me directly if there's anything you need or want. And again, you have my gratitude and that of the entire force. Great job."

"Thank you, sir. I'll report it tomorrow morning, but for now, that food and hot coffee sounds like the priority for me."

Danny, Tiny, and Angela accompanied Andrea in walking over to the back of a state police van, where the promised sandwiches, chips, donuts and cookies, and a couple of large carafes of hot coffee were waiting for anyone to help themselves.

Practically every member of the state police force at the crossroads found their way over to shake Andrea's hand, give her a slap on the back, and offer their respectful comments on her major collar. Danny, always her biggest fan, couldn't stop grinning in the background. Tiny and Angela looked at their best friend with great pride and love.

After eating and drinking and receiving congratulations for an extended period of time, Andrea kept protocol and rode back to the post in Traverse City in one of the patrol cars to check out for the day. Danny drove Tiny and Angela to the post for them to retrieve Tiny's Lincoln Town Car and head home to collapse, and after seeing them off, picked up Andrea, who quickly fell asleep as he drove her home and to bed

CHAPTER THIRTY-SIX

Even though Andrea was far too exhausted to make it to her choir rehearsal Thursday night at the Grand Traverse Presbyterian Church, the rehearsal of close to three dozen choir members became a beehive of comments as breaking news was spread about the arrest of the dreaded murderer of two state police officers and the kidnapper of a young woman from the other side of Kalkaska.

"And my nephew, who's a reporter for the *Traverse City Record Eagle*, told me that our Andrea's name is being mentioned as the arresting officer," one older lady in the choir shared freely.

"Our Andrea? From our choir? Really....?"

"I know she's a state police officer," a third lady added, "but I guess I assumed she mostly wrote speeding tickets."

"Imagine," yet a fourth chimed in, "a hero in our own choir. Do you suppose they'll have her on television?"

In the next two days the buzz around the congregation increased so that when Danny and Andrea met Tiny and

Angela on Sunday morning for worship, Andrea was virtually mobbed as soon as she stepped through the church door and into the narthex. She wished she could duck all the attention, but the good members of the congregation at the Presbyterian Church were sincerely proud of her and her colleagues in the state police, and they wanted her to know they were proud.

She grew a bit concerned that in having to say "thank you," and trying to explain that the apprehension of the murderer had very much been a team effort, her voice was going to become hoarse for singing the choir anthem that morning. Word had also started to spread that Angela had played an important role in the manhunt, and people clustered around her, asking about what it was she had done to help catch the villain.

The pastor didn't want to put anyone on the spot, but thought it important to include in his pastoral prayer that morning "and we give thanks for those who serve and protect us, who put their lives on the line in standing against evil and violence, especially our police, firefighters, and civil servants who faithfully discharge their duties for the common good of all our citizens." By that time, everyone knew who he had in mind in his giving thanks.

Before the morning was over, both Andrea and Angela felt like slipping out and hiding until someone else took the spotlight for a "fifteen minutes of fame." But they were also grateful for the support, encouragement, genuine interest, and love that so many expressed for them.

"I have to tell you, guys," Andrea sighed as the four best friends sat down at a table in the Mackinac Brewing Company for an after-worship lunch, "if I had known about all of the attention and hubbub that was going to result, maybe I should have let Trooper Harding or one of the other pursuit team members take the collar and I'd just hide in the background."

"Nah," Danny rejected the idea, continuing to be as proud of his beloved wife as any husband could possibly be. "I know by now, love, that when you're on a sacred mission, nothing on earth can stand in your way. You were going to get your man, come hell or high water."

Angela chimed in, "And that Junior Smith was as evil as any demon straight from hell...and man, was there a lot of high water during that chase."

They all laughed heartily, with Andrea nodding agreement vigorously. Tiny had to add his immense pride in Angela's contribution to the successful chase.

"Now I know, brother and sister, how it is that Angela can always track me down, no matter where I've gone or what I'm doing." Danny and Andrea howled appreciatively as he went on, reveling in his own joke, but also turning serious for a moment, "But seriously, sugar, I didn't know you had that super-tracker ability..."

Andrea interrupted and spoke to the two men especially, "I kid you not, guys, this woman could follow an ant that walked across a mile of bare rock and scoop it up out of another thousand ants at its nest."

Angela broke into the torrent of praise with the most serious, deadpan face she could muster, "Well, actually, each ant leaves a faint but definite scent trail across any surface it travels. You see, there are these glands...."

"See what I mean," Andrea gestured toward her best friend, and Tiny roared, "That's my girl."

Angela turned actually serious for a moment, "That's what I did during so many of those summer visits to my grandma's Apache people in Arizona. Almost every day my cousins and I would play a kind of hide-and-seek out in the desert, but the challenge of the game was to employ every method possible to go and hide without leaving the smallest trace of which direction you had gone, or where you were hiding. The seekers, of course, learned over time from the very best trackers like my grams and my great-uncle Many Horses how to find the faintest tracks and trail left behind by the one hiding. It was great fun...although my cousin Harry Many Horses once stayed out in the cold desert for three days because he didn't want to be found and no one could do so. He won a big ice cream sundae for that one."

Danny had been laughing so much that he hadn't said much, but as Andrea and Tiny shook their heads, smiling, at Angela's story, he finally spoke up.

"Well, you two had better brace yourselves, because this adventure is going to be in the news for a while. And it will probably be resurrected at each major step of Junior and Wes Smith's pre-trial, trial, sentencing, and incarceration over the next who-knows-how-many months...certainly well into next year. And from what Lieutenant Wade told me, it sounds like there will probably be some award recognition for both of you."

"I just want to go home," Andrea winced, "lie low for a while, and go back to my usual duties. Although all of that drug raid preparation has already started to bear fruit, and I guess I'll be busy for some while with that."

"I agree," Angela added, "it's back to my bookkeeping and gift selling for this lady."

Tiny had been thinking as they were talking, "Do you suppose the state police would let you wear your uniform in my new ad campaign: *Tiny's Big Protect and Serve Comes to Your Home and Business*?"

Andrea's mouth dropped open, and Angela whacked him on one of his massive shoulders. "I'm just kidding," he assured them, "just kidding." But he moved a little farther away from both of them.

Danny offered a conclusion as they prepared to leave the

restaurant and go home for a Sunday afternoon rest.

"I have to tell you, I'm just glad there'll be no one else gunning for any of us after all this. Sarah and her brother Ken Romano were more than enough for me. And you, Tiny, don't need another Ken grazing your leg with a bullet. We won't have to have any more run-ins with Wes Smith. He'll be going away for a long time for his collusion with his murdering younger brother."

"Yes," Andrea added, "and I never want to see Junior Smith again, although I'll probably have to testify at his trial. I hope they lock him away in some dark hole and throw away the key."

"So, let's go home," Danny said as they headed out the door, "put up our feet, and thank God it's all over." The other three responded with an even heartier "Amen" than they had uttered just a little bit ago in church.

CHAPTER THIRTY-SEVEN

She sat down at an open computer terminal in the library and signed onto a news website. The years had taken a definite toll on her, and she looked older – more worn, wrinkled and haggard – than she should have in her early fifties. It seemed as though her short-cropped dark hair became increasingly gray week-by-week. A small but visible, ragged scar marred her left cheek. Her once-bright eyes were perpetually reddened and squinted.

She went to a favorite page of the website – Regional News in the *Traverse City Record-Eagle*. Her eye was caught immediately by a photo with the caption "Traverse City State Police Post Celebrates Winner of Medal for Conspicuous Bravery."

She squinted harder and scrutinized the photo and the article below it. Front and center in the picture was "Trooper Andrea Henriks, arresting officer of double-murderer and kidnapper, Junior Smith," being awarded her medal for bravery and distinguished service. And in the background behind her stood "the Rev. Dr. Daniel Henriks of the Presbytery of Mackinac."

The disgust and anger distorted her hardened face even more as she stared at the photo and article. *So, Daniel's little chippy is a big shot now, taking credit for a lucky arrest. And he's standing there, looking so smug and self-important. Damn them both. Goddamn them to hell for what they've done to me and my family.*

I suppose it was a mistake to have Kenny enlist our second cousin Smitty to help him ambush Daniel...and then his idiot younger brother gets involved and messes up the whole affair with his drug run. Stupid backwoods kid, killing a state trooper. And then a second one. And still Daniel Henriks is alive, thumbing his nose at me, so smug with his uniformed bitch.

Ah, maybe it's really my fault. You have a clogged sewer pipe, you need to call the pros to ream it out. Never leave an important job to amateurs. Death is too important not to have it administered by an expert.

She closed down the website, rose from her library chair, and called, "Guard." And Sarah Brand went with her escort back to her cell in the State Correctional Facility for another night alone.

The Angel of Providence and Protection surrounded Danny and Andrea that night as always. The two lovers and spouses slept soundly, feeling completely safe and secure. And they were, for a considerable time in the future. The angel would continue to watch over and ahead of them so long as it was God's will that it do so. It was not known in what time or season God's mind and will might change, or God's plan might send the angel in a different direction...only God in heaven knew that. As a pure agent of God's power, the angel did only what it was directed to do.

There was no capriciousness or element of chance involved, only what God decided had to be done. And so, Andrea and Danny, Tiny and Angela, had to be protected and provided for. They were truly, greatly blessed.

The End

EPILOGUE

Continuing the saga established by *Death Comes to the Rector* and its sequels, *Death Crashes the Wedding* and *Death Stalks the Forest*, Book Four in David Q. Hall's *Death Most Unholy* series in entitled *Death Not Investigated*. Below is an excerpt:

"Well, Chief Investigator, what do you think?"

"I think Jose was telling the truth about no one else getting sick - at least as far as he knew. But he got really agitated about your questioning regarding the wild mushroom appetizer. I seriously doubt that he was responsible for mixing a plate of such deadly poisonous mushrooms, but it could be he knows more than he was revealing to us. If those two dozen others had been served that toxic dish, there would have been an outbreak of sickness, maybe even a fatality or two, or three."

"And as you pointed out in Tiny's hospital room," Danny added, "what are the odds that all three of those deadly poisonous mushrooms, from different habitats, would have been accidentally misidentified and mixed together with edible varieties? Maybe one of them, okay, but all three? It was a truly evil concoction, undoubtedly meant to murder."

"But if it could have been a targeted poisoning," Andrea furrowed her brow again, "why Tiny? I could understand if I was the target - it could be someone I arrested in a drug raid, or some other perpetrator - but what reason would anyone have to murder him?"

"Andrea," Danny leaned closer to her and took her hand, "the wild mushroom appetizer was supposed to be for me. I passed it over to Tiny because there was more garlic than I like."

ABOUT THE AUTHOR

The Rev. Dr. David Quincy Hall is a retired Presbyterian pastor living with his beloved wife, the Rev. Maxine, their daughters, son-in-law, grandson, and two dogs in Oceanside, Southern California.

David is a lifelong civil rights activist, environmentalist, and social justice advocate. His first two experiences in pastoral ministry were in the inner-city areas of San Francisco, California and Pittsburgh, Pennsylvania in the 1960's. He has dialogued with and lobbied members of Congress in Washington, D.C. and state legislators and committees regarding these issues.

His parish ministry was with congregations across the country in Pennsylvania, Michigan, Iowa, Wisconsin and California, in diverse settings including metropolitan, inner city, suburban, medium-sized and small cities, small town, rural, and the North Woods. On a personal note, he has also has a lifelong love of Nature, forest, lakes and streams. The scenes, tracking details, and other outdoor facts come directly out of his own experience Firsthand experience living in those different areas provides rich and accurate details for the scenes and settings in his books. Even more, his privilege in working with and serving all kinds of people helps to create characters who are authentic and believable as you meet them.

Death Stalks the Forest is the third book of his *Death Most Unholy* series. The first book, *Death Comes to the Rector* was a bestseller in paperback fiction. The second, *Death Crashes the Wedding*, was published in 2019. The fourth and final installment in the Danny-Tiny-Sarah saga, *Death Not Investigated,* is due to be in print in 2021.

www.ingramcontent.com/pod-product-compliance
Lightning Source LLC
Chambersburg PA
CBHW020440180626
46812CB00003B/1325